LOSING MY RELIGION

by Kyell Gold

This is a work of fiction. All characters and events portrayed within are fictitious.

LOSING MY RELIGION

Published by FurPlanet
Dallas, Texas
http://www.furplanet.com

ISBN 978-1-61450-275-3
Printed in the United States of America
First trade paperback edition: September 2015
Cover and all interior art by BlackTeagan
"CryptCreep BB" title font by Blambot, *http://www.blambot.com*
"REM Orange" heading font by Positype, *http://www.positype.com*
"Gtartings" guitar icon font by Thamyris, *http://www.dafont.com/ michael-herndon.d1913*

For Trem and Kit, fellow fans.

And for Michael, Peter, Mike, and Bill.

Thanks for the music, guys.

Tour Schedule

Night 3: Begin the Begin

Staring out at the darkened parking lot through the windshield, I kind of wished someone would walk by as I came in my paw with a pretty solid grunt. Not theatrical, not like I was trying to draw attention; just the kind of grunt a coyote might give after he'd been thinking about his wife while he pumped himself off all over his fingers. And a little on the steering wheel. Well, I'd clean it off eventually.

"Jackson?"

The flutey voice from the back of the van was pretty soft, like he was trying not to wake anyone up, only I was pretty sure his boyfriend was awake, and he knew damn well I was awake. "Gimme a second," I panted, and gave another grunt, that one a little theatrical.

"Fucking hell." That deeper voice was Matt, the boyfriend. "You couldn't wait 'til we were asleep?"

"What," I called back, "you mean like at five this morning?"

That shut them up for a minute. Then Lars, in his soft voice, said, "Sorry. We thought you were asleep."

"Yeah, you thought wrong."

Matt chimed in again, with a growl. "For Christ's sake, Jackson, you're finished, put your cock away. Anyone could walk by."

I squeezed my still-hard knot and slid fingers up my shaft, brushing a couple leaky drops from the tip and shivering. "A, if anyone walked by, I could see them before they saw me. B, unless they were ten feet tall, they wouldn't be able to see over the dash to get an eyeful of my delectable length. The only reason you can see it is because it's reflected in the angled windshield, which brings me to C, clearly you're enjoying the view, and I shouldn't wonder it's probably the finest cock you've seen since...how long have you and Lars been exclusive? Is it a year now?" The big wolf started to growl something, and I hurried on. "D, if you'd come out to the bar to be my wingman tonight, I might be showing off privately to a lovely lady and not to you all, and E, most importantly, as you know, it takes us canid family males a little while to completely, shall we say, detumesce following an orgasm. So you have about ten more minutes of the Jackson Show. Enjoy it while you can. You too, Lars."

The arctic fox, of course, stayed silent, while Matt engaged with my banter. "Don't blame your striking out in the bar on me having a steady boyfriend. I don't see why you can't just jerk off in restrooms."

"What, you mean like Zeb?"

Matt hissed, "Jackson!"

"Easy," I said. *"He's* still asleep." I looked to the side and back, at the rail-thin kit fox curled in the back passenger seat, his fluffy tail curled up around his legs. His gleaming eye met mine, and I winked at him. He'd put his cock away, but I didn't know whether he'd finished or not. "What do you think he was doing for twenty minutes in that Chevron at Bolo Ranch?"

"I don't care what he was doing. You could've waited until morning. The stall at the Happy Donuts locks too."

"Yes, well," I waved my paw around, in case the scent wasn't strong enough. "Masturbation is what happens while you're making other plans. Anyway, I just can't fantasize about Jazmyn in a filthy restroom stall."

"Isn't that where you met her?"

"I met her in a spotlessly *clean* restroom stall, thank you."

Zeb had looked away, and now his head was down, his breath fogging the van's window. In the rear view mirror, Matt's eyes gleamed out of a wolf-shaped shadow over the dim white glow of Lars's head and ears. His head was lowering, and he said, "Well, just tell us next time and we'll leave you ten minutes in the van alone. And we'll do the same when we want some time."

My cock was still dripping, but I could feel it going down. I cradled its warmth in my paw, still feeling quite pleased with myself. "Sounds like a good ground rule."

"All right. Behave yourself, then."

His head disappeared from view. Lars's eyes stayed open for a moment, then closed.

So I grinned, slid down in the seat, pushed my rear up onto the steering wheel, and proceeded to lick my cock and paw clean. I don't know if anyone walked across the parking lot. If Matt was still watching, he didn't say anything. But when I looked back at Zeb, I saw the shine of one eye before the kit fox's head dropped quickly again.

Day 5: Talk About the Passion

We rocked this little club in San Marino, second show of the tour. The first one, back on day two, we'd been a little rusty, but this time we went through our set smoothly, and they applauded enough that we didn't feel like douches coming back out for the encore. We did "Find the River," one of my favorites in our repertoire, and a sentimental favorite of lots of R.E.M. fans in San Marino, judging by the applause it got.

I left the stage last, tossing my guitar pick to the crowd like my much-more-famous counterpart, and hurried back to the cramped dressing room. The first thing I saw was slim hips bending over with a fluffy tail curling around a tight little ass, and I thought, wow, lucky me, I bet Jaz didn't think I'd actually get any on the road. Then the hips straightened and I saw the bass guitar case the same time I recognized Zeb.

Well, shit. I just stood there with my guitar hanging out, until Matt came up to me and said, "Mind chilling here for a drink? Lars and I want the van for, oh—"

"Sex," I said, recovering my natural coyote poise. "We get it. Go fuck and be fucked." I made a sign of a cross in the air between us. "You have my blessing."

"Well, thanks," Matt said sarcastically, but Lars gave me a sweet smile and blew me a kiss.

"What they don't know," I said to Zeb as they walked away, "is that my blessing ensures them a grand old fuck. I'm like a god of eroticism or something."

He giggled and nodded at my guitar. "Put that away and I'll buy you a drink."

San Marino is a sleepy suburban West Coast town full of red clay roofs to make it look Old World and big chain stores to make it look modern. The club felt like something that had been here since the sixties, old dark wood and brass fixtures and grizzled, sun-bleached patrons who looked like a faded Polaroid. But the ambiance was fine and at least the first drink was on the house for the band.

"So," Zeb said as we sat at the bar, glasses cold in our paws, "does anyone besides me know you're a god of eroticism?"

I held my scotch under my nose and breathed in the mediocre six-year-old malt. With tonight's take, I couldn't afford anything better if I wanted to be able to buy a drink for a girl later. "Actually, Matt probably does know. I blessed him the first time he hooked up with Lars."

The kit fox flicked his ears and set down his drink, a club soda with a wedge of lime. "You guys have known each other a while."

"Oh, fuck, yes. Six years? Freshman year college. We were in a shitty band because we were freshmen and we thought we could play. I," I raised the scotch, "have gotten much better. Matt is still pretty shitty, you might have noticed."

"He plays okay," Zeb said. He bent his head and lapped at the clear fizzy water, and brushed the lime with his tongue.

"You're being diplomatic," I said. "He's an average drummer at best. It's okay, he really wants to manage. Lars wants to sing. I want to play. You clearly do, too."

He lowered his ears but smiled, like any musician when you compliment their playing. "I've got a long way to go."

"Yeah, so do we all. But I know how good I am, and I'm pretty good, and you're better."

He turned to the chalkboard that read, *Tonight: REMake.* "So who came up with the band name?"

"Actually, our first bassist, the one you replaced. It was originally ReREM." I spelled it out with a claw and condensation on the slick bar wood. "You know, like re-R.E.M., doing R.E.M. over again, and then if you spell it out…"

He mouthed the letters and gave me a blank look. I sighed. Not everyone can be a coyote. "It sort of sounds like 'are we R.E.M.' It's the kind of wordplay the band would've liked."

"It's clever, I like it." He smiled at me and didn't ask whether I'd come up with it.

"Deirdre said that if people have to think about a name, they'll lose interest. It has to," I snapped my fingers, "click. They have to know right away." I pointed at the chalkboard. "That one's not clever, but it's brilliant. Everything's right there. Remake, R.E.M. It says "R.E.M. cover band" better than just about anything else I've heard."

He tilted his head. "Yeah, I guess it does." He lapped at his club soda again, and I let the scotch roll over my tongue. It was about as shitty as Matt's drumming. "So what do you want to do after this?"

"After what? The tour?"

"Well..." He perked his ears and looked around the bar. "I mean, you said you and Lars want to play, and Matt wants to manage. I can't think of a lot of successful cover bands. But when I asked Matt about that at the interview, he just said..."

I put on my deep Matt voice. "'There are all kinds of new pathways opening up for success in the music business.'"

He laughed. "Yeah, more or less. So..." He rubbed a finger along his glass. "You buy into that?"

"Matt's a real 'one step at a time' guy. Solutions-oriented, he likes to say. Knock down the problem in front of you first. If he gets us those East Coast gigs, we might have some people come look at us. He tried to get a couple producers to come to our show here, but nobody bit."

"Really?"

"Yeah. I'm sure he didn't tell you because he doesn't like to get hopes up for something until he's sure it's going to work out. Which is overly cautious in a band that includes his best friend and husband; it's just going to make you feel excluded. So don't. I'm telling you, that's just how he is."

Zeb nodded, but without conviction. Well, I could work on making him feel like part of the band. I'd figured anyway that that'd be my job. "So," he said, "what kind of people?"

"What?"

"Would come look at us."

"Oh." I tipped back the rest of the scotch. "No idea. Matt knows what he's doing. I just wanted to get away and play real gigs for a couple weeks. Do something with these paws that doesn't involve hammers." I wiggled my fingers. "We toured a couple times last year, and it's fun, sort of like a camping trip with the guys, only you get to play music at the same time and pick up lots of girls—and boys if you like that—in bars. We can't do it that often, though, because we always lose money. Surprisingly, there are not thousands of people dying to see four random guys play the songs of an admittedly awesome band that had maybe three or four legit mainstream hits."

Zeb smiled. "Have you ever wanted to play other band's songs?"

"Oh, sure." I put the empty scotch glass down. "You only practiced with us for the shows. Matt and I played—well, shit. Allman Brothers, Talking Heads, Morrissey, The Manics, Van Halen, Westerberg, The Feelies..."

He laughed. "You just listed off like five of my favorite bands. What about U2?"

I wiggled a paw. "Too commercial."

"Oh yeah. The early stuff, though."

"Sure, the early stuff is okay."

We talked music until his club soda ran out. "You think it's been long enough?" Zeb looked up at the clock.

"Half an hour?" I shrugged. "I don't mind giving them another fifteen. I'm having fun."

"Me too." But he looked toward the door of the bar, and drummed his fingers on the bar top. "Hey, uh…I never said thanks."

"For what?" I knew, but I wanted him to say it.

His ears flattened. "The other night…when you, uh, I guess you heard me, and they did…I thought everyone was asleep…"

"Oh, you mean when you were jerking off and I whipped mine out to cover for you?"

His ears went completely flat and he mumbled, "Yeah."

"I beat your time, too. Did you even get off?"

He shook his head. "Why'd you…?"

"Ah, I was enjoying the show," he turned his head away again, ears flicking, "and then when you gasped, Matt moved around, and you looked pretty terrified when you heard him. He already knows I'm sleazy, so it wasn't a big deal. I've jerked off in front of him before."

"Ah huh." He shook his head. "I was going to say, why'd you say that about the gas station bathroom?"

"So they wouldn't think it was you. Also so they'd think you were asleep. Matt and I might talk about each other jerking off, but we wouldn't talk about someone else's onanistic pleasures in front of them. Not if they were awake."

"But I was awake."

"I was lying."

He tilted his muzzle, trying to work his brain around that. "Do you guys talk about me when I *am* asleep?"

I put on my best innocent look. "So out of curiosity, why did you jerk off in the van?"

"Oh, I just…" He stared down at his empty glass.

I signaled the bartender for two gin and tonics. Zeb protested, but I told him to try it, and he said he would. When we had our drinks, he picked his up, and gave me a sideways look to see if I were still waiting for him to answer the question. My ears remained perked, my smile politely welcoming. He sighed. "I just can't do it in a bathroom. It's…it's gross, that's all."

"That all?" I tipped back the gin and tonic. "Don't lap this stuff, by the way. Tip it. So what's the big deal about not being able to do it in bathrooms? If it were bedrooms, I could see…"

He tipped the glass, pouring the clear liquid into his muzzle, and his grimace changed to appreciation. "It's just…we're guys, y'know? We're supposed to just be ready to whip it out whenever."

"So the bathroom no, but the van yes?"

His ears had just come back up and now they dipped again. "I was thinking about…my ex-girlfriend and kinda sleepy, and everyone was quiet and I was…ready…"

"You mean 'hard.'"

"Yeah." He tipped back the glass again. "Is it supposed to get better the more you have?"

"Most alcohol does." I polished off my G & T. "Then at some point it gets a lot worse."

"So I hear." He tapped the polished wood with his claws, obviously working himself up to another question.

"Go ahead and ask whatever you want to ask," I said. "I mean, you've seen my cock and I've sort of seen yours. We're living in the same van for two weeks or four, depending on whether Matt gets those dates on the East Coast set up. Might as well get to know each other."

"Yeah." His ears dipped and I thought I saw his eyes flick toward my waist, but I might have been a little drunk at that point. "So you've known Matt a long time. You guys ever…I mean, before Lars…?"

"Ha." Well, okay, I guess there were some things I wasn't going to tell him. "Nah, I'm, well, straightish." Not a complete lie, more of an incomplete truth. There were some nights, more than a few if I'm being completely honest, when we both struck out in the bars, and then… "But we love music and the biz, and we did some stupid shit together in college. That kind of bonds you."

"Well, uh. I don't want to ask him, because it's a dumb question…"

"What?" I took another drink to encourage him to finish his, figuring that'd make him a little less hesitant about the questions.

"How do they do it?" He indicated the door through which Matt and Lars had left, and the parking lot beyond, and the van parked there in which Matt and Lars were probably currently fucking. Or maybe done by now, depending on how excited Matt was.

I raised my eyebrows and smiled. "They love each other. The rest is easy."

His ears went all flat and he mumbled, "No, I mean, like...like physically..."

"I know what you mean." Whoof. All right, this was probably worth blowing the rest of my drink budget for the week. I signaled the bartender for two more G&T's, same shitty gin. "Seriously, you got through college at Elmwood University without learning about gay sex? Did your school not have the Internet?"

He mumbled something about search histories and IT regulations and I waved him quiet. "Okay, it's really easy. I mean, I guess you're confused about the butt thing, but that's...you don't have to go there right away. I mean, you know how blow jobs work, right?"

"I...yeah. Uh. In theory." He poked that nose down into his empty glass, licked out the last taste of tonic, and then slid the empty across the bar and picked up the next one.

"Oh my, you poor deprived boy. Okay, well, boys have mouths too. So you just..." I put my finger in my muzzle and slid it back and forth. It tasted of the lime and dirt from the bar top, so I stopped pretty quickly.

His shoulders hunched and he looked all embarrassed, so I stopped, even though it was kind of cute. "Look, it's not that big a deal. If it bugs you, just don't think about it."

If it did bug him, he probably wouldn't be drinking with me after I jerked off in front of him. I looked again down his slender body. I really shouldn't be forward like this. It was hard enough being in a band with two guys who were fucking each other, and I didn't even know if he was gay or bi. I mean, he was curious about it, sure, but lots of straight guys were curious in that cautious "I guess anything that gets me off is okay but that's weird" way.

"It doesn't bug me," he said. "But...I mean, with two guys...?"

"Blow jobs are just casual," I said, and then I tipped back the last of my G & T's and "really shouldn't" turned into "what the fuck." I flicked my tail casually and said, "Hell, I'll blow you if you buy me one more drink."

Luckily, as I was drunk enough to make the offer, he was drunk enough to laugh at it. His giggle cheered me up, along with the warmth of the gin suffusing my fur. "What about your wife?"

The moment, if there actually had been a moment, was over. "Ah." I waved a paw. "She'd do it for free."

We went back to the van and knocked, and Lars and Matt let us in cheerfully. The van kind of smelled like sex, but nobody jerked off that night, least, not while I was awake.

Day 6: Radio Song

At a pause in the song, Zeb said, "You ever think about writing your own music?"

The van was "a-rockin" again—not literally, but Lars and Matt wanted to watch a movie on the computer and Zeb and I didn't want to, so the kit fox and I were sitting on the grass in a park in Mertolado with our instruments out. Guitars, smart guy. It was a nice day, the sun peeking out from behind clouds and then hiding again, people strolling nearby, but not so much as to bother us, a creek burbling along giving the air a nice water smell. I was practicing "I Believe" and he was doing the bass line along with me.

When we finished the song, I took a break, rubbing my fingers together. "Sure I have. I started writing this thing for Jazmyn, only it started to sound too much like 'Be Mine,' so I started over and tweaked it some."

"Okay." He grinned at me. "Let's hear it."

I shook my head. "Definitely not."

"Come on," he said. "I've seen your cock, remember?"

"That's different." I smacked the guitar with my palm. "This is *personal.*"

"Ha." He snorted. "I'll show you mine."

I waggled my eyebrows. "Seen it."

His ears folded back, but his grin stayed. He plucked a few strings and then laid down a catchy bass line.

I cupped my ears forward. "I know that. Wait, I heard it somewhere." I hummed along with the notes, and then snapped my fingers. "You played it at your audition."

He nodded, and let his fingers rest. "None of you asked me what it was."

"It just seemed so familiar." I shook my head. "You wrote that? What would you have said if we asked you?"

"I would've told you I wrote it. " Now his eyes rose to meet mine. "So?"

I sighed. "Fine." I closed my eyes and let my fingers pick out the melody. I thought about Jazmyn, the way she smelled in the morning before she'd put on her perfume, the way she smelled in the evening when her perfume miraculously remained strong but her shoulders were slumped, the way that even when she was tired, she managed that sparkle in her eye and that wag in her tail for me, the way she could polish my cock with her tongue, the feel of her breasts under my fingers...

My fingers were moving and I was getting hard all at the same time. The way I was sitting, my guitar's weight rested against my sheath, which just made it worse. I tried to focus on the other things about Jazmyn, the way her brown eyes looked into mine when we had those talks, the way she described the guy she'd picked up a month ago and what it was like to fuck him, how hot the sex was after that...nope. I adjusted the guitar and kept strumming. She was great to hang out and watch movies with, great to laugh at the TV with.

I broke off the song and used the guitar to hide my crotch. When I looked up at Zeb, he had kind of a faraway look in his eyes. I figured he was looking for a nice way to say the song sucked, so I just went back into "I Believe."

That jarred him out of it. A couple measures in, he picked up the bass and we ran through it.

"That was really good," Zeb said softly, putting his bass down.

"You were great," I said. "I'm getting better. I screwed up three times."

"Your song, I mean. The one for Jazmyn."

"Oh." I smiled, and my tail thumped the grass. "Thanks. It's just a little thing."

"Nah, I mean, it had a lot of energy. Like...I could really feel how you feel about her."

I wondered if he was hard, too, or had been. I couldn't tell from looking or from his scent, although the breeze was moving more from me to him. "I still need to polish it some."

"Yeah, but the structure's there. You just need to put the time into it." He tuned his strings. "She doesn't mind you leaving for weeks at a time?"

"Pretty sure I miss her more than she misses me. I mean, we got married young," when she thought she was pregnant, I didn't tell him, "and we're trying not to lose our youth just because we're married, you know?"

He plucked a few notes. "Play it again."

"Well, uh..."

"Come on." He grinned at me. "It's good, I'm telling you."

So I ran through it, and to my surprise, he jammed along with me, improvising a bass line that, if anything, enhanced the sexual energy. At least to my ears. Maybe it was just that all my memories of Jazmyn were sexual.

Or maybe it was that there was a little spark between me and Zeb. I gotta admit, I rarely look at guys that way (Matt doesn't count; he's a special case, and anyway, he started it). There was a bit of a vibe coming off him—no, that was silly. Probably just the conversation we'd had about sex combined with thinking about Jaz.

I wanted to keep jamming, though. So once my song was over, I started in with some Westerberg, and he picked it up right away and joined in. It wasn't anything we could do on stage, but it was a melody we had in common, and I felt another tick in the familiarity checklist. It was almost like I was putting a move on him. I wasn't going to sleep with him, though. Even if there was a spark, we could just be good friends. One couple in the band was enough drama. And Jesus Dog, imagine if Matt found out I was sleeping with a band member again.

"So how long you lived in Yerba Bay?" I shifted to a simpler Westerberg song, one I could play while also talking.

He matched my song without even flicking his ears, like he didn't have to think about it. "Four years."

"And where were you before that?" I was tempted to switch to another song, but all the other ones I knew required more concentration. I'd finish this one first.

He strummed and looked off away from the van. "Well, uh." He went through a whole verse of the song, and I was about to tell him he didn't need to tell me when he finally said, "I grew up in Bonneville."

My ears pricked up. Bonneville was a big city, but the main reason someone might be reluctant to disclose his association with that was the dominant religion. If he were still active, though, he wouldn't have been drinking last night. Nor, probably, talking so casually about gay sex, though it would explain his lack of knowledge. "Oh. Were you…?"

"Mormon? Yeah."

"But not any more?"

My whole experience with religion was a year and a half between my eleventh birthday and my thirteenth birthday when my mom dragged me to the Christian Reformed Church down on DeAngelo Street. I think she was worried because my dad gave me a pack of condoms for my eleventh birthday, but she shouldn't have. Not one of those condoms went inside a girl; I wasn't nearly that precocious. I did jerk off into every one of them, but that wasn't 'til I was twelve, and the Christian Reformed Church wasn't so tough on masturbation anyway.

I swear, not every story of my life revolves around sex. That Jazmyn song was still on my mind, I guess. The point is, giving up going to church for me was as simple as Mom saying, "You don't have to go anymore." But I got the sense from the weight Zeb gave his words that it hadn't been so easy for him, and my question had maybe been too casual. So I said, "You don't have to talk about it."

"It's not a big deal." The words didn't quite convince me, but I let them go. "I just stopped going to temple a couple years ago."

"Elmwood corrupted you, huh? Was it the Yerba clubs or the campus bars? Or your fellow music students?"

Half-back ears, ghost of a smile, still not looking at me, still not missing a single note. "I thought, how can I know if I'm truly of this faith unless I try being without it? So I tried." A few more notes.

It wasn't a real answer, but I didn't know how to ask him what had spurred his questions. "Must have been rough," I said. "Your family okay with it?"

He shook his head slowly, ears flat, eyes down, and the smile was as gone as water in the desert. "Haven't talked to them. I mean…since then."

I felt like when I would try to talk to Jaz about female issues except worse, because she either got angry or laughed at me. She never looked like her best friend just pissed on her lunch. So I mumbled, "Sorry," and switched to "Man on the Moon" rather than opening my damn fool muzzle again.

The bass line for that song was tricky and malleable like the guitar chords, but Zeb spoke lightly, halfway through the verse. "It's okay. I'm dealing with it, y'know? It was a decision I made."

I nodded, screwed up the fingering, and focused back on the song. I was trying to compose a reply in my head, but just then Lars came walking across the park and sat cross-legged with us. He cocked his ears and then started to sing in mid-verse. "*Andy did you hear about this one…*"

A couple people tossed coins in Zeb's open case near us. When we finished the song, Lars wagged his tail back and forth across the grass.

"Movie over?" I asked. The air had cooled as the sun sank.

He nodded. "Matt wanted some peace and quiet to do some accounting. Let's do another song."

I met Zeb's eyes, and his smile held nothing but enthusiasm. Lars started us with, "*That's great it starts with an earthquake…*." And damned if we didn't make enough for a pizza dinner that evening.

Day 8: Pretty Persuasion

I couldn't *not* have alone time with Zeb, because Matt and Lars wanted alone time so often. I could've gone off on my own, I guess, but I'm a social guy and I didn't want to abandon the kid in the little shit town we were in. So at least I made sure we brought our instruments and practiced, because then I could keep the conversations light and bring them back to the music.

Tonight, though, we'd had a pretty good show, and Lars nailed it. He knew it, too, and he and Matt practically had their paws down each other's pants backstage, Matt murmuring in the fox's ear how *good* he'd been and how *sexy* that voice of his was, until I said, "Jesus Dog, you two, either get your clothes off and fuck on the floor already or go to the goddamn van."

Matt didn't even look at me. Lars giggled, and the two of them scurried out the back door, big wolf holding the arctic fox's tail. I shook my head and closed my guitar case, and when I looked up, Zeb was watching me. "Couple drinks?" he asked.

Well, I couldn't think of a good reason not to except that I couldn't really afford it, but this club had offered to comp us beer. Besides, I was starting to get that edgy, restless feeling in my sheath, and it's easier to pick up a companion for that kind of activity if you're drinking. "Sure," I said, just as I spotted a trio of bobcats down at the other end of the bar. My pickup history with felines is worse than any other group, but I pointed them out to Zeb anyway. "Hey, did you ever go out to bars in college and pick up girls with your friends?"

I had this idea that maybe I could get a wingman back, now that Matt was permanently grounded. But Zeb's ears folded down. "Not really."

"Watch and learn," I told him. Maybe in a couple stops he'd be a better one. I was seriously hoping to get laid on this tour and we were over a week in and it hadn't happened yet. I was pent up and running out of time, and annoyed at Matt. It wasn't even like I was asking him to be in an open relationship with Lars or anything. Just wanted him to come out with me for a few drinks and help me put the open in *my* relationship.

But right away I was off my game, because I wasn't flush enough to buy drinks for all three of them. And you can't just pick one or two out of a group of three; chances are they'll all get pissed and go, plus you miss your chance at a three-way maybe. Three is also tricky because they might just be hanging out together for the evening A girl by herself is probably at least open to a quick hookup. A trio is a lot less likely.

"Have you had two girls at once?" Zeb asked me when I told him this.

"Uh." I scratched my ears. "Not technically. Jazmyn used to have this one friend that she stripped with, and I watched them do stuff, but she didn't like guys. The friend, I mean."

He shook his head. "Lots of my college friends talked about seeing two girls together. I dunno. I, uh…" He lowered his voice and looked around as though someone from his family might be listening. "They showed me porn once…is it better in real life?"

I laughed, still trying to work out in my head how I was going to make my limited budget buy drinks for three girls. "Porn is always better. Real life is messy and sloppy and you're worried about getting the sheets dirty, and you have to go to the bathroom and she ate something that didn't agree with her, and sometimes your timing's off. But watching Jaz with Desiree was pretty cool." I turned to his ear and said, very softly, "And they didn't mind if I jerked off while watching."

He twitched, or at least his ear did. "That time in the van," he said, "that was the first time I ever…I mean, with someone watching…"

The way he said it, the bashful admission, sent my brain on a couple leaps of logic. "Hey," I said, "Have you ever? With anyone?"

"Yes," he said, and gulped at his drink.

"Okay." I dropped that subject in the face of his awkward discomfort. So, the girls. The obvious move was to introduce ourselves as part of the band—that's why you join a band, right? But it'd be a lot better if we could get them to notice us first. Otherwise we look desperate.

I kept glancing over their way, keeping my muzzle in a carefree coyote smile, which always works in the movies, not so well in real life. I knew that the one in the green dress was looking at me, but her friends were absorbed in a conversation.

"So how do we get them to notice us?"

"Usually we'd send them a drink."

He took another sip of his, making it last. "Bribe them, you mean."

"Well, yeah. If you spend money on them it shows you're serious. I guess." Honestly, the buying-a-drink had worked for me maybe one in two times, and only once since Jaz and I opened up our relationship. But that was likely just because I was rusty, and I'd been on my own. "Here's the other thing: we talk each other up, right? So if one of them asks what I do, you talk about how well I play guitar."

He nodded. "Be your wingman. I know about that from TV."

"Good. Okay, so…" I tapped my muzzle. Even though the girls had finished their drinks, they were still around. There weren't any other eligible guys at the bar, so I had to think they were interested in us. But how to…

Zeb was humming something under his breath. It took me a second to realize why it sounded familiar—the bass line he'd been playing with my song for Jaz. And then I had it.

"Wait here," I told him. I finished my drink, slid off my stool and padded around the bar to the bobcat in the purple bow.

The girls stopped talking as I came around. Besides the one I liked in the green with the moderate chest and the sweet smile, there was Zeb's target in the purple bow, and then the third one in the forest green shirt and pants who was going all country with her outfit, the shirt unbuttoned down to the cleavage and the pants ripped in strategic places. To me, it just looked trashy, and anyway, she was too top-heavy for my taste.

"Excuse me," I said to the one in the purple bow, "but my friend over there is trying to write a song about you, and he asked me to get your name."

Yeah, it was cheesy, but they giggled, and she told me her name was Violet (really?) and the one I liked was named Amaris and the one with the cleavage was named Penny. "You're in the band, aren't you?" Amaris asked.

So I called Zeb over with our drinks, and told them how awesome his bass playing was, and he said nice things about my guitar playing that were less true, and it turned out they were interested in talking to us (and maybe more), so we all retreated to sit around a table.

Amaris sat next to me, and Zeb squeezed in between Violet and Penny. The girls all worked at the Wal-Mart down the road, and when they told us, Zeb made the mistake of saying he was sorry—liberal education has that reflex action when faced with Wal-Mart. Fortunately, they didn't get angry, just puzzled. Nervous laughs to each other and then Amaris saying that all that stuff in the papers about Wal-Mart was made up by ex-employees with a grudge.

I couldn't figure out a way to tell Zeb that we weren't looking for fiancées and neither were they, so I just agreed that Wal-Mart had a lot of bad press, but that if the girls liked it, it was probably okay and I didn't have any personal evidence to the contrary. I dumbed it down a bit because we were in Shithole Central, and the girls relaxed. Penny did say, "We do what we have to," with a thoughtfulness that would've led me to reconsider my choice if we *had* been looking for fiancées.

To my surprise, Zeb bought the next round. He had a credit card he hadn't used before, and I wondered briefly why he wasn't helping us maybe rent a hotel room once in a while. Then I squashed that thought: he had no obligation to put any more into the band than his time and music, and he was obviously okay sleeping in the van. Maybe it was a credit card for emergencies, and he felt this was a time to be a little more spendy.

It worked; the girls got pretty loosened up. I had my arm around Amaris by the time her cocktail was half gone, and she scooched closer to me. Zeb kept both his paws on the table wrapped around his glass, though he smiled at the girls on either side of him and they liked him pretty well. I figured even if Zeb was shy, we could get the other two to come along if Amaris and I were getting along.

And we were. She dropped her paw to my thigh, and I leaned my thigh in closer. She took advantage, tracing claws boldly across my jeans and finding my hard-on. It was pretty clear she thought the same of me that I did of her, and was anxious to get down to business, but she still hesitated there, to give me the chance to push her away.

Which I didn't take. I mean, seriously. I was enjoying Amaris's exploration even through my pants, and the movements of her fingers left me little doubt that she knew her way around a cock. I slid my paw up her side to the curve of her breast to let her know that I had some familiarity with female anatomy as well, and we kept up our polite conversation while our paws did their own not-so-polite one.

Things were going pretty well until we finished that round of drinks, and we were all a little tipsy—the girls more so than we, because they'd started sooner and Zeb wasn't drinking alcohol. I can't even remember how we got on the subject. Maybe Amaris said something about how with canid males, you could tell the length of other things (with a squeeze to my "other thing") from the length of their ears.

I was a little distracted by the squeeze, so I didn't respond right away, and Zeb jumped in. "Oh, in Jackson's case that's true," he said.

Violet and the other one, shit, I couldn't remember her name, they both turned to him with their little ears perked. Amaris's paw stopped.

"You know each other pretty well, then," Violet said.

"Well, nah, not really." Zeb went on cheerfully. "But you know, living in close quarters in the same van, you see stuff."

Now Amaris took her paw away. Violet and Number Three looked at each other past Zeb's muzzle. "You guys...live in a van?" Amaris said.

"Just for now." Our nice pleasant evening teetered on a precipice. My mind tried to race ahead to figure out a way out of this, but two gin and tonics dragged me down. "You know, the glamorous life of a rock star, ha ha."

"And you sit around naked in the van?" Number Three chimed in.

"Hey," I said, "We're guys. We do disgusting guy things, you know? But not all the time."

"So," Amaris said, "when this bar shuts down, you guys were going...back to the van?"

Zeb, bless him, was trying to play along with me. "We'd be much better behaved with you around."

"I hope not," Amaris purred, and her fingers touched my thigh again.

"But," Number Three persisted, "you were going to take us to a van?"

"We can't, actually," Zeb said, "because the other guys are using it."

Ah, shit. Before the girls could say anything, I jumped in. "We were hoping to go back to your place."

Not very smooth, but I had to say something or else Zeb was going to keep talking. And how was I to know that they all still lived with their parents? What kind of town was this? Amaris lifted her paw again, and this time it didn't come back.

God dammit, I was still hard when I watched the three of them walk out the door. I didn't have the energy to respond politely when Zeb, ears flat, said, "I guess I didn't do so good."

"No," I said, getting up, and stalked out to the van.

I opened the door without checking to see if Lars and Matt were done. It had been over an hour, so fuck it, they oughta be.

"Hey, Jackson." Matt's voice carried a tone of warning. "We didn't come out—"

I spared him a glance. He and Lars were under the sheets, probably still naked, but at least not fucking. "You're done, aren't you?"

"We—"

"Because I need the van. You can stay and watch or you can get out."

And I sat down in the driver's seat, slumped down, and pulled my aching erection out of my pants. Jazmyn, I thought, kneeling in front of me with her tongue, holding me with her paws…

"Give us a minute," Matt said sharply. "We're not dressed."

I barely listened to him, already working my shaft. I wasn't even thinking of Amaris, just Jazmyn. God, what kind of mistake did I make, agreeing to this trip. Weeks without her, while she's fucking other—no, don't think about that. When I get back she'll be mine again, she'll be so happy to see me.

After some frantic movement behind me, the van door opened. I prepared to relax and lose myself in my fantasy. And then: "Jackson?" Lars's soft voice.

"Leave him," Matt said, louder.

Lars's paw landed on my shoulder. He said, "Hey, are you okay?"

"Lars!" The paw disappeared, but I could feel Lars behind me and it was interfering with my fantasy of Jazmyn.

"I'm fine," I snapped. "I'll be a lot better once I finish jerking off. So if you're not going to help, leave me alone."

"Okay," he said, and brushed my shoulder again. The van door closed, and I was left alone with Jazmyn, finally.

And still, it took me a good five minutes or so to work myself up to the edge. I pounded and gasped and came into her—my—paw. And then I meant to clean up, I promise, but I just wrapped my sticky paw around my warm shaft and let the tension drain out of me. And the next thing I knew, Matt was shaking me awake and telling me to go clean myself up.

Day 11: How the West Was Won and Where It Got Us

Zeb avoided me for a couple days, flattened his ears whenever I looked at him, and generally moped. Yesterday I let him, and it was easy because Lars and Matt didn't demand any time alone. So I talked with them and even though I kinda knew we were making him feel like the new guy, I was still mad at him and I didn't care. Lars tried to include him a couple times because he's like that, but Zeb just shook his head and retreated into his book or phone or whatever.

By this morning, I was feeling bad about Zeb. I mean, I did over-react, or at least my cock did. But on the other hand, it had been a week on the road, and apart from the good-bye blow job I got from Jaz, it had been another three days before that since I'd had sex. Ten days is way too long to ask a guy to go on just blow jobs and jerking off. And now it was thirteen. I went out the night before on my own, but without having just played in the club, nobody would believe I was a guitarist.

Aaaand I kinda missed Zeb.

Okay, there it was. I was trying to pick up this tiger, and yeah, she was way out of my league, but there was something else missing. Don't get me wrong, I was looking forward to getting her in bed; she was hotter than the desert we were stopped in the middle of. But the night before, I'd also been enjoying showing off to Zeb, maybe getting him laid too.

It wasn't that the most critical part was missing, really. I was just thinking that it wasn't as much fun as it had been, and then I was trying to figure out why, and around the time the tiger looked at her phone and said she had a job to get up for in the morning, I realized that if Zeb were with me, I wouldn't have to walk out of the bar alone.

He was already asleep when I got back to the van, and Lars and Matt were talking quietly in the back. So I just curled up in the driver's seat and shut my eyes.

And when we stopped for lunch, the day I started feeling like I should say something to Zeb, Matt held me back as Lars followed Zeb out of the van. He waited until they were out and then opened his long black muzzle.

"I know what you're going to say," I said. "I'm going to apologize to him."

"We have a show to play tonight." Matt leaned in close. "We all need to be up for it."

"We will be." I watched the kit fox walk away. "What's special about tonight?"

He shook his head, getting a smile. "It's going good, this tour, huh?"

"Going good for you. You get to play and have sex every night."

Matt's ears went back. "There's more to life than sex."

"Jesus Dog, Matt, you know I don't get to play around much at home. On tour is where it all happens. And without the rest of the band, I'm just a skeezy heading-toward-middle-age guitar player."

"For fuck's sake, Jackson, you're twenty-five." His ears went back. "Though you don't act it."

"Would it kill you to go out with me one night? Come on, we were so good together. Zeb's a sweet kid but he is not ready for active duty yet."

The wolf shook his head. "I'm not doing that anymore. Just go clear things up with him."

"Look," I said, "he may not know his way around a bar, but on stage the kid's a pro. On his worst day he plays as good as we need him to."

"Yeah, well." He clapped me on the shoulder. "We need him at his best. And for whatever reason, he's taken to you out of all of us. So go make nice."

"I was going to anyway," I insisted as we climbed out of the van. "You don't have to keep telling me."

"What'd he do, anyway?"

We locked the van and walked across the parking lot to the taco stand. "Ah, he told some girls we're living together in a van and that he saw my cock."

Matt stifled a laugh. I elbowed him. "The one girl had her paw wrapped around my business and we would have been doing the fur-to-fur dance if he'd just kept his trap shut. And because I know you're going to ask, yes, there were multiple girls and yes, he could totally have gotten one if he wanted."

"Fine, fine." Matt snorted. "Just take care of it."

So after a quick lunch of crunchy tacos that were pretty amazing, and a short conversation with a couple bears who wanted to know what four foxes (!) were doing traveling around the country in a van, Matt said he and Lars wanted the van for just ten minutes.

"We do?" Lars looked surprised and put a paw to his stomach, but Matt dragged him out of earshot before he could say anything else.

I elbowed the kit fox. "What do you think they can do in ten minutes?"

He didn't say anything, or at least not anything audible to sharp coyote ears, and I sighed. "Look," I said, "Zeb." He still didn't look at me and his ears didn't come up. "I'm sorry I've been a dick the last day or so. I got all worked up and...sometimes my dick talks louder than I do. It—"

"No," he said. "I wasn't upset at you. I was upset at myself. I should've known better than to say that. About the van, and about—"

"Hey." I played with the paper taco wrapper, shredding it with my claws. "It was your first time, and I should've been a lot more understanding. I fucked up. It's just..." I crumped the wrapper. The kid had probably not had a lot of action, so he couldn't really understand looking forward to it so much after months of occasional sex with Jaz and hearing about her other lovers, of striking out in bar after bar. "It's in the past, it's done with. Next time you'll do better."

He nodded, but stayed quiet. "And I really liked jamming with you."

That perked his ears a bit. "I liked it too," he said.

"I'm sorry," I said again, and put my fist up. "Friends again?"

He eyed the fist. "Can we have a signal? If I'm about to say something stupid—if I start to say something stupid—you give me the signal and stop me?"

I laughed. "Only if you do the same for me."

His eyes got a bit wider. "You?"

"It's been known to happen" I said. "Usually a few G&Ts in."

Well, that got him to laugh, so we got up and started walking back to the van. "Oh," he said, "has it been ten minutes?"

"Relax." I grinned and threw an arm over his shoulder. "Matt was just leaving the two of us time to talk. He and I are on the same page a lot of the time."

"Did everyone notice?" His ears were going down again.

"It's kind of hard not to, when we're all living in a ten by five van. Don't worry about it. Shit happens on tour, and we just deal with it and play the shows and move on."

I put my hand on the door handle and just then, both my and Zeb's ears perked up. A moment later, the moan we thought we'd heard sounded again, Lars's high-pitched breathy one.

I met the kit fox's eyes and we stepped back from the van. Well, nobody said Matt wasn't an opportunist.

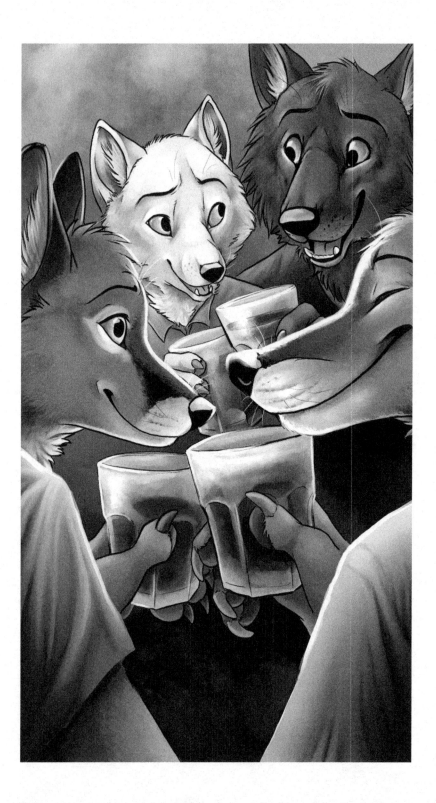

The show went off great that night. Lars wasn't quite fuck-me-after-the-show good, but he was good enough and he walked offstage with a big smile. Anyway, Matt wasn't around. He disappeared after the show, so Lars and Zeb and I sat around a table in the bar and celebrated with a bottle of whiskey the club manager had given us. It was as cheap as you might expect, but it was still better than we were used to, a name we recognized from commercials. Zeb, of course, stuck to club soda.

Lars and I'd gotten pretty nicely buzzed when Matt came back; we cheered him when he sat down with us. "It's the drummer!" I said.

"It's my hot boyfriend!" Lars said, and raised his glass, leaning in to Matt.

Matt accepted his glass and raised it to us. "It's my awesome band," he said. "Cheers to us, boys, we're going to the East Coast!"

The words took a moment to sink in, and then we raised and drained our glasses and all started asking questions at once. "Whoa, whoa." He pushed his glass in. "Hit me again, I gotta catch up. I'll tell you all about it."

So it turned out that the guy Matt had been talking to on the East Coast had seen a blog review of our second show and left Matt a message to call him tonight. They'd signed the deal: a dozen more clubs up and down the Midwest to the East Coast, starting a week from today. So instead of four more shows and done, we were going to do four more shows and then have to drive all through a night and a day and the next night, and then ten more shows in seven cities.

I used the pay phone at the bar to call Jaz on our cell phone. "Hey, babe," I said. "Good news and bad news."

"Oh," she said. "Go ahead."

"Well, the bad news is that I'm going to be gone another two weeks. So sorry to deprive you of Jackson lovin' for even longer, but the band's got the East Coast booked! We're going to Aventira, Port City—well, Shambletown, it's right outside Port City—and Peco and Freestone and all."

"That's great." She delivered that line with all the emotion of a porn actress.

"Hey, babe," I said, "I'm sorry, but I'm sure you've got plenty of company, right? That real estate guy still around?"

"Yeah." She seemed to recover herself a bit. "How about you, Jackson? Finding any company out there?"

"Ah, I tried, but it didn't work out. Playing all these shows, it's exhausting."

"How's the new guy?"

"He's—he's good. He's really good."

"That's good. I'm really glad for you guys."

"Thanks for understanding, Jaz."

We talked a little longer and then I had to go, because we were all heading back to the van to rest up for the next day—three hour drive and then a show, and another four hours and a show the following night before we started out for Aventira. I tucked myself up in the driver seat, curled my tail around myself, and thought that things couldn't possibly be going better.

Day 14: Just a Touch

Matt took the first shift out to Aventira, which was great because it gave me a break from driving the damn van. He and Lars sat up front and I was going to just crash in the back seat, but they nagged at me to use the bed and when I complained that it smelled like them fucking, Matt said he had spare sheets. Spare sheets! Where did he pull those from?

Anyway, with fresh sheets, I couldn't resist, and as long as I didn't stick my coyote nose into the middle parts of the bed, I didn't smell sex. Don't get me wrong; it was their bed and I didn't mind them having sex in it or leaving it smelling of them. And I was tired enough that I only stuck my nose in the middle of the bed once, just to be sure, and then my head hit the pillow.

Maybe it was sniffing Matt and Lars's sex life but I woke up from a half-dream of Jazmyn where I was pulling her against me—not sexually, not in the dream, but as the growling of the airplane we were riding first class in my dream shaded into the growl of the engine and the hum of the road, I found myself holding Jazmyn pretty close.

Only of course, you've already figured out it wasn't Jazmyn. I had my nose buried in Zeb's shoulder and just as the airplane became a van, my wife became a kit fox. I pulled my arm off him and edged back, only then becoming aware that I'd been rubbing my erection against his tail.

Maybe he hadn't been able to feel my hard-on, if it was just against his tail. I squirmed around and gave myself a little more space. From the light outside, it was early afternoon and I probably had a couple more hours to sleep before Matt would want me to take over. I wasn't all that hungry. Had I slept through lunch?

While I was still half-muzzily pondering the state of my stomach, Zeb shifted. His paw slid back along his own tail, and then, uh. There's no way to sugarcoat this. He reached back and groped me.

Yeah. If Matt had surprised me with the sheets, this was ten times, a hundred times more shocking. This was—this was unprecedented.

Or it would've been, if his paw had actually started rubbing and whatnot, like—well, like Amaris did when she found my cock and knew what she wanted to do with it. But Zeb's paw froze, and I didn't move, imagining him going through the panicked "oh shit what am I touching" even as he pulled his paw back.

He didn't move after that, leaving me plenty of time to shift my thoughts from "when are we going to eat" to "what is going on with this fox." Was he gay? Was he straight but interested in me because, let's face it, I was attractive and we were thrown together by circumstance? Or was I just reading into a shy, somewhat socially awkward guy trying to make friends, reacting to the admittedly fairly sexual nature of my life?

Hell, I missed Jaz, for sure, but lying next to him in the bed, I figured if he were gay, or interested in me, then let it not be said that Jackson Alley was unwilling to help a youngster find his sexual path. I wasn't going to shack up with him, and I think he understood that well enough, so if he did really want to play around, then, well…Jesus Dog, I was still hard, and actually staying hard thinking about Zeb rather than Jaz. Desperate indeed.

At least I could let him know that I wasn't upset. So I turned back onto my side and let my paw fall on his tail, under the covers where Matt and Lars couldn't see it. The fluffy thing twitched but didn't move otherwise, and I dozed off again like that.

It was still light when the stopping of the van woke me. I was lying on my back, Zeb stirring beside me but not touching me. I would almost have thought that I'd dreamed the touching incident, except that when Matt said, "Hey, you sleepyheads, you hungry?" Zeb just rolled out of the bed and climbed into one of the passenger seats without looking at me, his ears flat, fur all mussed. He groomed himself while I sat up in the bed and did the same.

"What's for eats?" I peered out the window, but from the bed, I could only see roofs.

"Your pick." Matt turned to grin at me. "Burgers, tacos, pasta, pizza…I found a shopping center that has it all. Lars and I are going to grab a salad. You want that?"

"I'm in a pizza mood, I think," I said.

"I'll get salad." Zeb still didn't look back at me, but took off with Matt and Lars.

Well then.

The pizza was delicious, for the record, and I offered to drive while Matt and Lars slept off that heavy salad. This led Matt to suggest we buy whatever we wanted to eat for dinner here and then just eat on the road, and mostly out of inertia, we all went along with him.

Loaded with sandwiches and a burrito for later (hey, they are just fine cold), I got us back onto the interstate. Matt and Lars went to cuddle/

nap in the back, and Zeb at first sat in the back until I told him to get up front and keep me awake, and then he slunk guiltily up.

I turned up music until I was sure Matt and Lars wouldn't hear us, and then I said, low, "Hey, don't be embarrassed about touching my junk." He struggled to pretend that wasn't what was bothering him. "Oh, God, did I? I, uh, I didn't realize—I mean—"

"I know you didn't mean it," I said. I checked out of the side of my eye, but he still wasn't looking at me. "I mean, if you'd meant it, you woulda given it a good feel, right?"

He made sort of a choking sound. I went on. "I get it, I do. You saw it the other day and didn't believe it was real. Had to find out for yourself. Believe me, I've been through that before."

Now he was looking at me, eyes wide, not smiling. "It was a mistake, I swear." His ears were still flat against his head, his whiskers down.

"I know," I said. "I told you, it's okay." I waited until his ears came up a bit, and then asked the big question. "You don't have to answer this now, but do you think you're gay?"

He opened his mouth and then shut it. "I don't know," he said finally. "I just always assumed I liked girls because that's what I was supposed to like. I never really got close to anyone before."

"You've never…" He was shaking his head even as I was saying it. "Whoo. Okay. Well, when you realized what you were touching, did you…like it?"

"No!"

"Thanks."

His ears flicked again. "I don't mean it like that. I mean, I was just so *mortified*, I didn't even think about…" He took a breath.

"Okay, well, what if I told you it was okay? Would you want to do that again?"

He stared out the windshield at the highway. "I don't know," he said again.

"If you do decide to," I said, "Just give me some warning."

Then he gave a short, nervous laugh, and I had to be happy with that.

So yeah, seven hours later, Matt finished up his dinner and took over driving while I sat in back to eat my burrito. Zeb sat next to me and joined in our conversation about the music Matt had put on. He and I had had some good talks and some good silences over the course of the drive, talking about the country we were driving through. A lot of it was near where he'd grown up—Mormon country—and so he told me the history he knew.

It was pretty interesting, and it passed the time. On and off, and especially as I finished up my burrito and got closer to lying down on the bed again, I wondered whether he'd been thinking about groping me, if he was going to try or if he'd be too embarrassed. He wasn't giving me any indication, so as my dinner settled and my eyes started to drift shut, I said I was going to go back and get some rest.

Matt said he'd wake me up whenever he got tired, which would probably be after midnight but before dawn, and I said that was fine. I crawled back to the bed, and Zeb didn't come along. I did take my pants off this time and stretched out under the covers intending to wait until he came back, but the next thing I knew, the van was dark and I was blinking sleep out of my eyes.

Zeb was there beside me, but not close or anything. I shifted, freed my tail from below my hip, and lay on my side. No dreams this time, but I was still hard just from being asleep. I stretched a paw down to feel myself, and found the tip of the kit fox's tail there, too. So I brushed it with my fingers, cupping my ears to listen to the sound of his breathing, slow and rhythmic. I could hear it easily even over the music and low conversation from the front of the van. Still asleep.

I used to listen to Jaz this way, although I also used to tease her awake and I didn't want to do that with Zeb. As hard and aroused as I was, I knew that most of it was just from not having gotten off with someone else in a couple weeks. And Zeb was a good kid, curious but shy, and if he didn't want his first gay experience to be with me, I certainly didn't want to push him into it. It was funny; Jaz, when we'd opened our relationship, had asked me if I wanted to play around with boys. I said that if a really hot one came along, I probably wouldn't say no, but I wasn't really about to go looking. In retrospect, she probably asked because she'd feel a lot better if I were just messing around with boys. She knew that I wouldn't leave her for a guy.

Zeb had a nice, soft tail. Not as soft as Jaz's, but pleasant to run fingers through. I fell into a doze, dragging my claws through the fur, and blinked back to wakefulness when the bed shifted and bright eyes shone back at me.

"Sorry," I whispered.

"Don't be." He stifled a yawn and then looked steadily at me.

"Sleeping well?"

He nodded. His eyes turned away from me for a moment, then back. He parted his lips, said, "Uh," and then I waited for what I figured he was going to ask. "So, uh," he whispered, and glanced toward the front of the van. "Uh. Can I?"

In response, I reached out and took his paw, but he pulled back. "I can, uh. I can find it."

His fingers reached out to my thigh and then found the edge of my boxers. He closed his eyes, but I didn't, watching his expression as light from the oncoming headlights washed over it, bright for a second, then dark again. His paw rested on my hip and then slowly, tentatively, lowered.

By then I was all the way hard and out of my sheath; I mean, try not getting aroused when someone's lying next to you in bed and has announced their intention to grope you. Okay, no. I don't mean it like that. Well, maybe I do, sort of; trying not to get aroused could be fun— "nope, I'm hard, let's do it again"—but I just mean that I was thinking about fingers on my sheath and that meant my cock was feeling fingers on it before they got there, and so when they did finally get there, they found warm hard readiness.

Ready for what, I didn't know. He pressed through the boxers, trailing up the hard ridge, and found the edge of my sheath where my cock was exposed. He hesitated there again for a moment, then went all the way up to the tip.

Once you've touched a guy's cock, it becomes a lot easier to touch more of it (having something to lower your inhibitions helps if it's a first time, like alcohol, or being half-asleep in bed next to a guy, I guess). He seemed enthralled: his lips parted and he scrunched his eyebrows like he was really concentrating. I wondered whether his other paw was comparing himself to me. His touch was nice, but after several strokes up and down I was feeling more teased than anything else, and he wasn't making any move to get inside the boxers. So I pushed them down.

His paw snapped back at my touch, but he figured out what I was doing and reached out again right away. This time, after sliding his pads up my skin (surprisingly sensual; I had to stifle a moan), he actually circled my cock and held it in his paw.

We lay like that for a while. I wanted him to start stroking, and I felt like I should be returning the favor somehow, but I didn't want to spook him, and I was kind of afraid that his shyness was just lurking, waiting to reassert itself. Also I didn't want to finish in the bed while Matt was driving. I mean, apart from the fact that I'd already been snide at him for doing exactly that, I would then have to sleep in messed-up sheets.

Anyway, it was kind of nice lying with Zeb's paw around my shaft, and the rumble of the van provided a little stimulation. And then he started moving his paw up and down.

I let out a breath in a long hiss. I should tell him to stop. I would, in just a moment. I could stop him in time. It usually took me a minute or two to jerk myself off. I could stop him in time.

I could—

"Sss," I hissed, and pressed my muzzle into the pillow.

He stopped, which was what I wanted and did not want, and I groaned my frustration into the pillow, possibly loud enough to be heard over traffic and music, I couldn't tell. My cock was hot and pulling my own paws down toward it, my blood pulsing and singing and I knew I shouldn't finish, should tell him to stop, but his paw was still around it and it felt warm and good and I couldn't tell him to move it, not when it was right there already and fuck, what the hell was I going to do?

"Sorry," he whispered back. "Should I not? I don't know…" And he started stroking again.

Oh God. Oh God, I wasn't going to stop him in time. I guess now at least I knew what I was going to do.

My whole body shook, and I reached out for him and got my paw in his fur, and he edged closer and his paw kept moving, stroking in that rhythm and my cock was on fire, my whole groin was sparking, and then I jerked my hips hard forward, and I was spurting all over the sheets, and I tried not to moan, but a little got out and I spurted some more and the tension raced through me from ears to tail and then was gone.

And without the arousal, my brain started working again. My first thought was that now Zeb and I could ask for alone time in the van, but then I remembered the fox's worry and hesitation, and that didn't seem like a commitment he'd want to race into. He was hesitant enough about sex that he might not even want them to know he'd just jerked me off. But Matt and Lars would know in a minute regardless. So…Jackson to the rescue. I lifted my muzzle, trying to get to his ear, but it turned into sort of a nuzzle, which he half-returned. "Jump…out of bed…" I panted. "Act disgusted. Like I was…doing myself."

"Uh-uh," he said, but then I felt him sniff against my fur.

"They'll smell it in a minute. I'll take care of it," I whispered. "Go. Go."

He let my cock go. I hoped he didn't have any come on his paw. Then his warmth was scrambling away from me, up into the rear passenger seat.

"Hey there," Lars said. "Couldn't sleep?"

Before Zeb could reply, I gave a throaty moan. "Oh, Jaz!" I threw the covers back so they'd catch the smell and grabbed my still warm cock, now dripping on my fingers.

I kept my eyes closed, but I'm sure Matt and Lars were both looking back. "For God's sake," the wolf said, with fangs in his voice. Lars didn't say anything. "Is it too much to ask that you not jerk off for two fucking days?"

I didn't give a shit. The smell of sex overwhelmed me and I lay back, letting Matt's words wash over me. "Apparently," I murmured, and let the post-orgasmic bliss carry me away.

Lars said something conciliatory, but I didn't catch the words. I was drifting off when something brushed my ear. I turned and found Zeb's tail there. When I looked up past it, the kit fox's eyes gleamed down at me. So I gave his tail an affectionate squeeze and drifted off to sleep.

Day 15: All the Right Friends

Zeb brought me a beer from the corner store down the street from the Laundromat. "Thanks." I toasted him with the bottle, which was one of the cheaper light beers. "Sure I can't pay you back for it?"

He cracked open his ginger ale and sat next to me, taking a drink before picking up his bass. "I owe you."

I grinned at him. "I feel like I owe you."

"For covering, I mean." He peered at the washers. "Twenty more minutes?"

"And then probably an hour in the dryer. Matt and Lars should be done by then, but they'll probably stay in the van anyway."

He gulped down some ginger ale and then picked up his bass. My guitar sat next to me, but I didn't feel like practicing. "So, uh, did I do that good?"

I snorted. "If you couldn't tell…"

"I mean, I don't know." He plucked a few strings, just randomly.

"Okay." I sipped the beer and grimaced. "I didn't intend to finish. I just got carried away. So yeah, you got me carried away. That was good." He didn't say anything, so I nudged him with an elbow. "Was it good for you?"

His ears flattened and this time when the thought crossed my mind that he was adorable, I let it stay. "I guess, I mean, it was weird." He looked around, but the Laundromat was empty; several washers and dryers were going, but the patrons didn't stay to watch them. It was that kind of neighborhood.

"How different was it from jerking yourself off?" He was getting used to me just putting things out there, I guess, because he didn't flinch at that.

He didn't answer right away, either, but he started playing the bass line from "Texarcana." I didn't feel like picking up my guitar, so my foot tapped the tile floor while he composed his answer. "See," he said, "I haven't done that all that much, so, uh. It was different, but I was hard, too."

"Wait." I set the beer down. He didn't stop playing. "What do you mean, you haven't done that much? Do Mormon cubs not jerk off?"

He didn't look at me. "Not when they get caught by their mother when they're twelve and get taken to see the ward bishop and lectured about how their body is a pure temple and they are wasting potential life."

"Oh, God."

"And given pamphlets. Which they were ordered to read with their parents."

My jaw dropped. "Good Lord."

"I didn't have a door on my bedroom until I went to college."

All I could do was shake my head. "I…I think I would've run away from home."

He did put the bass aside then. "I thought I'd sinned. I mean, it was painted out to me like I'd murdered all the cubs I could've been having with the…the stuff on my paw."

"Jizz," I said helpfully. "Spunk. Come. Semen, if you want to be clinical."

He wet his lips. "Yeah. So I was terrified. I thought I was going to court like a murderer if I did it again. I prayed every night for years for God to spare my soul. It was…"

"It was fucked up."

"Traumatizing. I mean, I got over it."

"Clearly."

"Mostly."

I leaned forward. "Hey. I don't want you to be feeling obligated to… you know…if it's going to fuck with your head. I'd rather have you as a friend and bandmate."

"Friend." He smiled, and his tail wagged, the first time it had moved since he sat down. "No, I wouldn't have offered if I wasn't curious. I went to a therapist at college for a couple years and I have some mental exercises I do, and I kinda wanted to…to challenge myself, you know?"

I smiled back. "I can't imagine jerking off *making* me tense."

"It helps that the body is, uh, designed to, y'know. Enjoy it." He folded his ears back but put them up again right away. "A lot of the exercises I was taught are about mentally relaxing, letting go. The body is supposed to take care of the rest."

"You did pretty good for not having a lot of experience." Part of that was probably that I was worked up and on a going-on-three-week dry spell, but when someone's gotten you off, even if it was just an awkward paw job, you say nice things to them. Especially if they might have hangups about sex.

"So, uh, it's okay with your wife? You're sure?"

"Oh, yeah." I leaned back. "We went open a while ago."

He plucked a few strings. "How does that work?"

It worked because not being open wasn't working. "Well, we were always kinda progressive. When we were apart—when I was out touring with Matt—it was okay for me to hook up as long as I was safe and didn't get anyone pregnant, and vice versa for her. Then last year, when Lars replaced Zach, Matt got serious about getting the band out on tour, and I was gone for three weeks here, two weeks there. So Jaz and I had a talk, and decided if we could be open when we were apart, we could do it when we were together too." And Jaz had already cheated on me once, so rather than put the burden on her to be faithful, we decided to be open. "It's tough, but not so bad if you love each other. You just have to communicate, and we promised to put the other before any of our hookups." Honestly compelled me to add, "Not that I had many to talk about when I wasn't out touring."

"So, like..." He flattened his paw across the strings. "Are you going to tell her about last night?"

"Oh yeah." I grinned. "Don't worry, I'll make you sound good."

"You said I was good."

"So it'll be easy."

He smiled, but didn't say anything. "One of the things about being open," I went on, "is that you trust your partner not to break the emotional commitment. I don't mind playing around with you a little more, or we could try to pick up some girls together if you want."

He held up a paw. "That's nice, but...one thing at a time, I guess. I just wanted to make sure I wasn't going to mess up anything with your wife."

"Nah, I love Jaz. I like you."

"And I guess..." He lowered his voice. "You're not a hundred percent straight."

I flicked back my ears and gave him a long coyote grin. "Who is, really?"

"I wouldn't know." He started to play again, and this time I perked up my ears, grabbed my guitar, and joined in.

The washer finished two songs later. I grabbed a rickety cart and wheeled it over. "By the way...do you care about whether the other guys know? What we're doing, I mean?"

He pulled a load of wet clothes and dumped it into the cart. "I don't know," he said after a few seconds. "But I appreciate you going out of your way to make sure they didn't."

"No problem. Is that it?"

He pulled one last bunch of clothes out. "That's it."

We wheeled the cart over to the dryers. "They already think I'm crude and sex-crazed, so it's not a stain on my character. I figured you can decide when you want to come out to them, once you get more settled about what you want to do and what you want other people to know. Maybe you are gay but you don't want to advertise it. Maybe you like being a little sleazy, but you don't want the reputation yet."

The squeaking of the cart followed us and then stopped as we found two empty dryers. I threw the wet clothes into the first one. "Thanks," Zeb said quietly. "It means a lot to me."

I reached out and wrapped an arm around his chest, and poked my muzzle at his ear. "Hey, it's what friends do for friends." I paused. "I didn't know how much you needed it, but I'm glad it worked out."

We sat back down, pulled out the guitars and started messing around on them again. I'm pretty sure it wasn't because of the paw job, but I was having a great time jamming with him. I'd never found someone I could jam with who was also reliable enough to be in a band. The best guy had been Ollie, a raccoon I'd actually learned a lot from, but he couldn't stay off drugs long enough to do anything with the talent he had. Deirdre left the band to spend more time with her boyfriend (sort of), our friend Bristol from college went into accounting, and our previous lead singer just wanted to be high all the time.

Zeb was different. When he played, he was not only thinking about what he was playing, but listening to what you were playing, and adjusting. He would take things off in another direction, but whenever he did, it would fit where you were going too. The thump-thump of the clothes in the dryer made a nice background to our playing.

"So," Zeb said after a bit. "If I don't want to tell the other guys yet… where can we have some privacy?"

"Well," I said, "We've established that you don't like restrooms."

I put my sleazy coyote mind to the problem, but before that, we had a show to do. We'd gotten to Aventira early enough to take that laundry break (sex break for Lars and Matt), and an hour or two later, we were practicing in the tiny room backstage. We'd gotten through the mainstays when Lars coughed and said, "Zeb, would you want to walk with me down to the liquor store and get some beers for later?"

The kit fox looked at me first, and said, "Aren't we, uh. In a bar?"

"They're cheaper at the corner store," Lars said.

"I want to stay here with Jackson and work on cues," Matt said, which was probably as transparent to Zeb as it was to me. I gave him a brief nod in case he wasn't sure if he should leave us alone.

When they'd gone, I set down the guitar and assumed my Serious Coyote pose, leaning forward, elbows on knees. "You don't really need to work on cues," I said. "You want to tell me to cut out the jerking off at inappropriate times in the van. Look, it's not the same as it was with Deirdre. I—"

I was going to tell him that I liked jerking off with people around, which wasn't entirely false; I mean, I can get off one way or another, but I kind of like shocking people. But Matt cut me off, shaking his head.

"Lars and I know that it's been tough for you. We have each other, Zeb is, I dunno, asexual or something," at which I hid a snort, "and you haven't exactly been setting the girls on fire between here and home. I guess without me to help, all you have left is your own charm."

I ignored that slight against my sparkling personality. "If you all pooled your money to buy me a prostitute," I said, "then I appreciate it, but I'd rather get through this on my own."

"Don't be silly. We can't afford a prostitute." Matt delivered the line with deadpan wolf humor. "No, Lars and I talked about it and we agreed that if you're really pent up and lonely, I can help you relieve some of that tension. Like we used to."

I squinted at him. I'll admit that even though I knew Matt pretty well, this possibility hadn't occurred to me. "You mean, like, with a massage, or are you offering to blow me?"

He flicked his tongue out. "If it'll keep Zeb from freaking out that he's living with a compulsive masturbator, I don't mind."

"I have a problem with almost all the words in that sentence," I said. "Does Zeb look like he's freaking out? He and I spent the afternoon together, you know. While you and Lars were 'relieving tension' together."

"I just want to make sure this East Coast swing goes well." He spread his paws. "Are you feeling okay? I mean, I thought you'd have your pants down within ten seconds of hearing the offer."

"What, here? Now?"

"Lars promised me twenty minutes. He says it takes him that long to decide on the right kind of beer anyway. I'm sure Zeb won't push him to decide faster."

I clasped my paws together. Matt was right: my inclination when offered a blow job was to open my pants and lean back. But I was hesitating, partly because I was wondering if I had an obligation to tell Zeb.

Then it occurred to me that after my conversation with Zeb, I wouldn't need to whip my cock out to cover for him anymore; we'd be planning our alone time better. So I could let Matt blow me, and claim that had relieved my 'compulsion to masturbate,' as he would have it (honestly, what guy *doesn't* have a compulsion to masturbate, I'd like to know). He'd be happy he'd found a solution, I'd have gotten a blow job (a pretty good one, if I remembered right)…everybody wins. And if I had to tell Zeb, well, I'd tell him. I didn't think he would be shocked.

"It's very noble of you," I said, unfastening my pants. "But are you sure twenty minutes will be long enough?"

He smirked and came forward to kneel in front of me. One large black paw grabbed the waist of my briefs and yanked them down over my sheath. "If it isn't," he said, "I'll let you fuck me."

Well. Suffice to say, I did not get to fuck him. Even if I'd wanted to, he was good with that tongue and the paw, and Jaz's good-bye blow job being but a distant memory, I coated the inside of his muzzle pretty quickly. But it was purely physical; there wasn't anything like I shared with Jaz. It was just, as he'd said years ago, a couple friends swapping bodily fluids.

He spit into a cup and left to flush it in the bathroom while I lay back and thought about what a pretty good life I had, and also about how this dressing room would be a good place to be alone with Zeb if Matt and Lars wanted the van after the show. I thought about Zeb's muzzle on my cock, and about mine on his, and our paws in each other's fur. It was a couple friends swapping bodily fluids, that was all, except that me being his first and all, I felt kind of privileged, and responsible for showing him a good time.

Matt sprayed the room with floral Neutra-Scent and I got my sheath tucked away. "Thanks," I said. "That was swell."

He snorted. "If you'd fuckin' ask, I wouldn't mind it once in a while."

"I only need it on tour."

"It's not about what you need. That is a whole other mess that'll take more than a blow job to fix."

"Hey," I said, cocking an ear, "isn't that Lars and Zeb coming back?"

It wasn't, but it forestalled Matt's whole "you can't have both a family and a band" lecture, and it wasn't actually long before the other two returned, so he just thought I had super-amazing hearing, which I do. Until Zeb joined, I had the biggest ears in the band.

Of course, my life can't go perfectly even for one entire day. Despite our practicing, Matt and I were tired from the trip and the driving, and he missed some of his riffs, and I fumbled once and lost track of "Daysleeper" because we'd only added it for this tour. The crowd was forgiving, but not enthusiastic, and so partly because we weren't happy with the show, and partly because they'd already fucked that afternoon, Lars and Matt did not retreat to the van, and Zeb and I did not get the dressing room to ourselves (even though I'd already had Matt's muzzle that day, the prospect of some time with Zeb excited me, and I wanted to maybe tell him about Matt—if not the blow job, then at least that he'd talked to me about the jerking off). Instead, the four of us sat in the van and drank beers and played through the bits we'd messed up, and then went to bed.

But as I was dozing in the driver's seat, a paw reached around to touch mine. I clasped it gently and heard a soft sigh from Zeb, and that's how we went to sleep.

Day 16: The One I Love

Fortunately, the second show was also in Aventira, in another suburb, so we didn't have to get up at any particular time. We lazed around that day, and just to prove that not all of our lives revolve around sex, we found a used record store and wandered around looking for anything rare and interesting. Didn't find anything, but we had fun showing each other the things we already had.

It was just outside the record store that I saw the pay phone and decided to call Jaz, check in, maybe tell her about Zeb and that I missed her. The other guys had spotted a pizza place down the street, so I told them I had a call to make and waved them in.

"You're in Aventira now, right?" she asked when we'd said our hellos. "How is it there? How'd the show go?"

"It's awesome. It's chilly, and the show wasn't our best, but it went okay enough, and we're just going to grab some pizza. How are you?"

She was quiet for a bit. "Jaz?" I said.

"I'm pregnant," she said.

This was huge. I mean, the whole reason we got married was because she'd thought she was pregnant. Really thought, too, not just a trick to get me to marry her. I don't think she wanted that any more than I did when we did it. But we did, and then she wasn't pregnant, and we could've split, but we liked each other enough to keep trying. We tried monogamy, and slowly learned how to talk to each other, and then we tried an open relationship, but keeping her time in season just for me. So far, she was happier than she'd been in years, and that made me happy, too. And now we were going to bring a cub into that family.

I was having trouble finding words. I think I said something like, "Amazing," and how I thought she'd been close to going into season that last time, and then she cut me off.

"And I want a divorce."

I don't remember a lot of the rest of the conversation.

Zeb came out to get me. "Hey," he said, running up, "the pizza's out, and—Jackson?" His muzzle swam into view. "Jackson? What happened? Are you okay?"

"I'm fine," I said automatically.

"Well, come on. The pizza is…" He closed a paw around my arm. "You're not fine," he said. "What happened? Who'd you call?"

I was leaning against the wall that divided the pizza restaurant from the dry cleaner next to it, and the smells of tomato sauce and detergent assaulted my nose. Across the narrow street, people walked hunched against the wind, ears as flat as mine, tails tucked similarly under their coats. Had they all had bad news? Was this a particular street in Aventira where bad news gathered? That had been my mistake, turning onto this street.

"Jackson?" Zeb's voice softened.

"I'm fine," I said again. "I don't want to talk about it."

He sighed. "Come in and have pizza. It's cold."

Eat? I was vaguely aware of a gnawing where my stomach was. "Is there beer?"

"Yes." He tugged on my arm.

"All right." That was what I needed: something to blur the memory.

So I stumbled along the pavement after the kit fox, and as the warmth of the pizza restaurant washed over me, redolent of tomato and cheese and garlic, I breathed in and realized I needed to collect myself if I wanted to avoid having to explain to Matt what had happened. I squared my shoulders and marched back to the booth where they were sitting.

"Who'd you call?" Matt asked, eyeing me. I slid into the booth and Zeb sat down next to me.

"My mom," I said. "Just wanted to see how she was doing."

Zeb shot me a weird look, but didn't say anything. I ordered a pint of beer and then sat in my corner and nursed it as quietly as I could while Lars and Matt talked about the different pizzas we had back home.

A couple times that afternoon, Zeb tried to get me alone, but I stuck grimly to the others. Here, I was still part of something and I didn't have to imagine returning home to an empty house.

Pregnant with someone else's cub. Had she done this intentionally? She hadn't said, only that—from the pieces I remembered—there was a guy, a coyote, the one she'd been fucking before I left. I thought it'd been a little close to her season, but I'd trusted her. She didn't know if she loved him but she wanted a family. She loved me—in a way. She was sorry.

I wanted to call her back because I hadn't listened closely enough. What if we stayed married, but the cub went to live with his father sometimes and came to live with us? I could live with that, couldn't I?

Maybe she hadn't suggested that because she hadn't thought of it. If I called her—no, I couldn't call her. I knew better.

Still, I kept staring at Matt's phone and remembering that Jaz and I shared a phone, and getting sidetracked wondering if I would keep the phone, if the father of her cub had one he was going to give her. And then I didn't want to start thinking about that, so I just looked away.

Somehow I made it to the show. Matt pulled me aside in the back room next to the bathrooms before we went on and said, "You going to be okay? You've been weird since you talked to your mom."

"I'm fine. I'll be fine."

"Okay. Because we can't postpone this show, but the three of us could manage without you. Zeb can play guitar if he needs to."

It was tempting, but I also knew if I took him up on it, I would just start sinking into depression. I needed to take my mind off of things, and I had to play, so I would play. "I'm fine," I repeated. "I can play."

He looked me in the eye. "Anything you want to talk about?"

What the hell. "Jaz is leaving me." I figured I'd leave out the part about her being pregnant, for now.

His eyes widened. "Ah, shit," he said. "Shit. I'm sorry."

He tried to put an arm around my shoulders and I shrugged it off. "We can talk about it later," I said. "I'm okay to play."

"Jackson—"

"Jesus, I'm fine. I mean, I'll *be* fine, and it doesn't affect my playing anyway, okay? You can't fix everything."

His ears flicked back and his brow lowered, and then he remembered that I'd just been dumped and he got sympathetic again. He patted my arm and said, "Okay, but if you need to talk, I'm here. We can get some time alone."

"If you want to blow me again, just say so." It was unfair of me, but I was angry and frustrated and it just came out.

He did the ears flicking again, back and then forward, and then took a breath. "This is me, Jackson. Tell you what, I'll buy you a bunch of drinks after the show and you can forget about her for a couple hours."

"Fuck that," I snarled. "Drinking isn't going to help. Let's just play this show and get it over with."

His long nose stayed right up next to mine. His eyes bored into me. "All right," he said finally. "But after the show, you and me are going to have a talk, and a couple drinks."

When I didn't say anything, he brought his paws up to my cheeks and patted them. "I know it ain't much, but you've still got me. And Lars, and Zeb." He snorted. "If he doesn't quit the band from you whipping out your cock in front of him every few days."

That, of all things, stopped me. "I'll be better about that," I said. "I'm not really feeling like whipping it out now."

"Don't worry." Matt gave me a sympathetic grin. "I'm sure you'll be back to the same old exhibitionist coyote in no time."

I wasn't so sure, but I at least felt good enough to go out on stage. That, in retrospect, might have been the stupidest thing I did on the whole tour, including getting jerked off in Matt and Lars's bed.

There are some guys, and I bet Zeb is one of them, who can play through anything. They might've broken up the day before or gone to their mom's funeral or something, and they still can go out and hit every single goddamn note. I thought I was that kind of guy, but no, not so much.

I fucked up on two of the first three songs, and Lars picked up on it. He messed up one of the verses, and while I don't think the crowd caught my mistakes—or else just put them down to "that guy on guitar is kind of shitty"—they sure as hell know when you sing the song wrong.

A couple people laughed, a few people left, and Lars got rattled. Even though I got kind of shocked out of my funk and didn't seriously fuck up after that (I missed cues on two more songs—D- performance on this show), it was too late. Lars stumbled halfway through "It's the End of the World As We Know It" and more of the crowd turned back to their own conversations, more left, and a couple hooted.

We finished that song, and Lars stalked off the stage. I had my head down, but I heard Matt go after him. Out of reflex, I waved to the crowd and trudged offstage. Zeb followed me off, but we'd barely gotten out of sight before we ran into the club manager, a short weasel.

"You can't stop," he said in a shrill voice.

"Case you didn't notice, we're short a lead singer and drummer." I tried to push past him.

"Not my problem." He stepped quickly to block my way. "You guys are contracted for an hour and you've been out there forty-five minutes. You give me at least fifteen more minutes or you get zero money."

I was about to tell him how little I gave a shit, but then he added, "*And* you're gonna be billed for the beer."

Well, shit. I didn't mind losing money we hadn't gotten, but I didn't want to pay money for playing a gig. I turned and looked at Zeb. "I guess we gotta go back out without a singer. You know 'Tricycle'?"

He shook his head slowly. "But I can pick it up."

"All right," I said. "I can stretch that out to seven minutes or so. Then I can maybe piece together 'New Orleans Instrumental' enough to close out."

"Let's do it." He clapped me on the shoulder.

"Tricycle" is a fun repetitive track, but I got bored of it pretty quickly. Zeb picked it up, of course, and then I sort of remembered how "New Orleans Instrumental #2" went. The thing is, R.E.M. wasn't big into instrumental tracks—most of the ones they did were non-album tracks—and I hadn't bothered to learn many of them. And I sure as hell wasn't going to try singing.

The manager tapped his watch as we finished up and held up five fingers. Well, shit. I looked at Zeb, and he looked back at me, and then he stepped up to the empty microphone.

I thought at first he was going to sing, but he just said, "Ah, we're going to close with an original song. It's inspired by R.E.M. We hope you like it."

The two people left paying attention applauded. I frowned at him, mouthed, "What?"

He stepped back and fingered a few strings, and then he started playing a jazzy little bass line. It took me a second to recognize it, and then I lifted my paws from my guitar and shook my head violently.

Zeb just kept playing, his eyes pleading with me. Christ, of all the things to do to me, what was he thinking? I couldn't play Jaz's song, tonight of all nights. But he ran through his bass line once and then started in again, and my fingers dropped to the strings. I couldn't help it; the melody wanted to be played. So I played it.

And I played it pretty well. It's my song, so I get to play it however I want, but I mean, I played it the way I'd been practicing it. The first few measures were hard, because I was thinking of Jaz, feeling her arms around me, thinking how I'd probably never get to feel that again. I maybe held a couple of the notes a little longer than I should've.

But Zeb's bass line picked me up. He reminded me that there were other people, that my world wouldn't just be Jaz and our never-to-be cub. I'd played the song for him, where I'd never had the nerve to play it for Jaz, and now he was playing it back to me.

I wasn't going to forget Jaz over the course of one song, but for the moment, I was focused on the kit fox with the bass guitar. I played the song for him and for the audience, and by the time we finished, we'd gotten one or two more people to applaud.

The club manager was clapping too, and ushered us off the stage. "You boys did great," he said. "You ever want to come back on your own, just call me."

I gave that the half-second wave it deserved and hurried back after Zeb into the storage closet/back room that we'd been given for preparation. I kicked the door shut and just stood there.

"Sorry," Zeb said, "but that was pretty good, wasn't it? I mean, it was—"

I crossed the space between us in a long stride and grabbed him, pressing him against me and kissing him on the lips.

It was just a quick kiss, you know, a "holy shit good show thanks for stepping up" kiss, but when I did, he stared up at me and then he pushed his muzzle forward again and then I was tongue-kissing another guy for the first time.

You wouldn't think that was a big deal. I mean, I had Matt's cock in my mouth, for fuck's sake. But that was just sex, just playing around. This was—this was beer and music and a kind of togetherness that we'd just shared out on the floor. Love? Maybe in the moment. Not what I had with Jaz, whether she wanted to admit it or not, but maybe that wasn't love either. I wouldn't know.

But anyway, the tongue thing felt weird, and not only because Zeb wasn't very good at it. He was kind of trying to lick my mouth or something in that I've-seen-this-in-the-movies-but-this-is-my-first-time kind of way, and the only person I had to compare it to in the last few years was Jaz, and I did not want to think about that. So once the flush of the kiss had passed, I pulled away from him and touched my nose to his.

"Thanks," I said. "I needed that." And then, because his eyes were still kind of dazed, "The music, I mean. Not the kiss. Though the kiss was pretty nice too." Little lie to make him feel better. Although when he pulled me against him, I felt his hardness against mine and realized that maybe it didn't matter how good the kiss was technically: it *had* been good.

"Uh," he said, and he was grinning now. "Can we stay in the room here for a bit? They won't come back?"

"Fuck 'em if they do," I said roughly, and dropped my paws to his belt. *And fuck Jaz*, I said in my head. *I don't need her.*

"Hey," he squeaked, and wriggled.

"It's fine," I said. "It'll be fine. They're probably fucking in the van and the manager doesn't want to see us yet. Probably hopes we get more beer."

"But, uh." He squirmed away from my paw. "I mean, I was just thinking we could kiss for a bit more…"

My cock throbbed. "Look, I'll put a chair on the door." I grabbed one of the big, heavy wood chairs and jammed it under the door handle. They did that in movies all the time. I had no idea if that shit actually worked, but it looked good. "Okay? Even if they come back, they can't get in."

"Then…then we'll have to explain why we blocked the door…"

I reached forward again. "My wife's leaving me," I said. "I told Matt about it. So I'll just tell them I don't want to be disturbed. We good?"

"Uh…" He lifted his short muzzle and met my eyes. "I'm really sorry. Are you sure—"

The compassion just made me want to kiss him again. "This'll help. But if you don't want to…"

"No, I do."

"Good." I unfastened his pants and pulled them down. While he was kicking them off, I cupped my paw around the thick shape of his sheath and balls, rubbing through the fabric. "I want to fuck, somehow."

"You can fuck me if you want." His voice stayed low and quiet.

That was hella tempting. I reached around to feel his butt, and he had that great firm curve that early-twenties guys have even if they don't work out so much. Mine was lean, but I was already losing definition from being in my mid-twenties and married. I'd never fucked a guy, but imagining it made my already-hard cock even tighter. Still, there was a problem. "No lube here, unless the club provides it. Might be lube and condoms in the bathrooms."

"I could check." His eyes were wide and eager, a little scared but hell, it would be his first time.

Was it worth it? The upside was, well, obvious. The downside was that it would take five or ten minutes and we might lose the moment. And, my mind said in a desperate attempt to reassert reason over the turmoil of emotions fucking with me, Zeb was diving headfirst into the deep end of the gay sex pool, and if I wanted to be his *friend* and not just his first fuck, my obligation was to ease him in and make sure he didn't drown. Also this shitty little dressing room would be a lousy place for his (and my) first time. "You okay with just blow jobs?"

He nodded quickly. "Sure."

"Okay then." I slid my paw into his boxers, which made him squeak again. He was all the way out of his sheath, hard and warm under my fingers. I pressed him up against the wall and kissed him again as my paw worked his cock, making him moan into my muzzle.

"Mmmf." He had his paws on my hips and kept them there, though his fingers trembled toward my tail. You'd think, having already jerked me off, he'd be less hesitant about grabbing my butt, but Mormon upbringing, I guess. So I gave him a little more tongue and little tighter grip on his cock, until he shuddered and pushed me away.

"You okay?" I grinned at him, my tongue hanging out.

"Uh." He panted. "Yeah. But. Isn't, uh. Isn't the point of a blow job to, y'know, uh." He licked his lips. "Not finish in paws?"

I nodded. "All right. Let's get to the 'blow' part then."

"Wait, wait." I'd hooked my fingers into his waistband and started to pull. "I, uh, can I…?"

His paws moved from my hips to the front of my pants. "Sure," I said.

"I mean, I'll still be ready in…in a bit, but I might not…after I finish…"

I reached down and unbuckled my pants for him, exposing the goods. "There you go."

He looked for a long time. "Hey," I said, "if you were gonna wait this long, I could run and get a condom."

"No, no." He rubbed his paws along my stomach and then dove down into my boxers, finding my shaft and curling fingers around it.

I rested my paws on his shoulders. "Mmm. It hasn't changed since the last time you touched it."

That seemed to help. "I know." He looked up at me shyly and then stroked with a little more confidence. It didn't take long before I'd pushed my pants all the way down, but when he got on his knees, I sat down as well.

He tilted his muzzle questioningly and I dropped back to rest on my elbows. "I don't like being on my feet."

"Okay." He bent over me, taking my cock in a paw. I gasped as he drew his tongue along the tip. "Uh," he said, "am I doing this right?"

"Yeah," I said, curling my claws into the carpet. "Oh yeah. I mean, if you just jerk me off with your muzzle at the end, and keep doing ah-ah-yes that…" I clenched my jaws and moaned through my teeth as he took my advice.

And of course, it was right when he had my whole cock in my mouth and his fist tight around my knot, with the pressure surging in me and the voice in my head reminding me that it was the kid's first time and not to jam my cock down his throat, that three sharp raps sounded at the door.

Zeb's tail got all frizzed up, and he practically fell off me. Cold air hit my cock, and I rasped, "Go away!"

"Jackson?" Matt's voice was accompanied by more knocking. "Hey, I finally got Lars calmed down. Why's the door locked?"

I motioned to Zeb to be quiet. "Because I didn't want anyone coming in here. You know how locks work, right?"

"Uh…okay. Where's Zeb?"

I met the kit fox's eyes, which were wide and scared, and gave him what I hoped was a reassuring smile. "Fuck if I know. We finished the set and he just took off. I thought he was out there at the van with you."

"We haven't seen him. I'll take a look around." The door handle jiggled again. "Are you okay?"

"I'm fine! I'm having…some private time, okay?"

I heard him breathing, and then he said, "Sure. Just come find us at the van when you're ready."

Thankfully, he moved away after that. I rolled onto my side and reached out to Zeb. "Sorry about that," I whispered.

He nodded. "Can't he smell me in here?"

"Yeah, but the dressing room smells like all of us. I mean, if you'd come on the floor or something, then he could smell that, but…nah, he'll just think it was residual from when you were here before." I thumped my tail. "Okay?"

Again, he gave a quick nod. "Okay." His eyes flicked down toward my groin. Neither of us was as intensely urgent as we'd been just two minutes before. I was definitely still worked up, though, of course. "You want me to finish?"

I lay back on my back and exhaled. "If you want. I know the mood's kinda gone."

"I feel bad leaving you like that, though." His fingers brushed my shaft, making me shiver. "And you did tell Matt you wanted some private time."

I closed my eyes, remembering Matt's tongue. Two blow jobs in two days? I definitely deserved it, and the warmth in my cock at that thought indicated that my body agreed. "Well, I think the mood can come back."

It did, and though I didn't say anything to him, the idea that Matt might come back and find me with my cock in Zeb's mouth absolutely did not hurt one bit. Also if I thought about being the first one Zeb had ever sucked off, that helped too. And the warmth of his fist around my knot, even though he wasn't really that good with his tongue yet, got me off pretty fast.

"Unh," I said, gesturing, remembering at the last minute to warn him. "Zeb. Zeb! Ah!"

It was just at the wrong time, as I shuddered and bucked, and he pulled his muzzle back the second I came. This time, I barely noticed the cool air on my cock, just the heat inside me and the spurts in time with my moans, spattering Zeb's chin and whiskers.

"Ah," I gasped again, fists clenched, "unh, sorry!"

He made a noise and just stared at me, his paw still tight around my knot, muzzle slightly agape. I watched a small drop of my seed drip from his chin to land on my hips.

"Uh," I said again. "Sorry."

He lifted his free paw to his muzzle, then stopped, still looking at me. "I…" He glanced at the door and whispered, "I'm a mess."

"Some people like that." I lay my ears back. "Uh, you can come on my face if you want."

He shook his head and didn't smile. "I'd rather just clean up."

We both looked around the little closet-cum-dressing room, where four chairs and one dresser and no sinks crowded around us. "The bathroom's just down the hall," I said. "I'll wait 'til you get back?"

I made it a question deliberately, and he shook his head. "That's okay. Maybe another night." Slowly, he got to his feet. "But…what if Matt comes back around and sees…" He gestured to his muzzle.

"Well, okay." There was at least a box of tissues on the dresser, and I reached up to grab one so I could wipe myself a bit clean. I offered him the box, but he shook his head.

"All right." I stood, and got an idea. "I can…"

I leaned forward, and he recoiled. "What?"

"Hold still." I reached around to the back of his neck and brought my muzzle forward.

He squirmed, but I managed to lick a bit of his muzzle clean. It wasn't as good as when it was warm, but it was my mess. "You don't have to—" he protested, and then shut up as I licked around his lips.

"If I'm not willing to have it in my mouth, I shouldn't have sprayed it on yours." I kissed his nose and winked, and then licked up the other side of his muzzle. "I'll go back to the van first. Matt and Lars will expect me to smell like sex, and I'll keep them there until you clean up and come back. Deal?"

"Mmf." He nodded as I finished up licking, and then folded down his big ears. "Sorry."

"Hey, it was your first time...I think?" He nodded again, one quick one. "You did great. You'll get better with practice."

"Did you enjoy it?" he asked softly.

"Hell yes." I snorted. "There's not really such a thing as bad sex. And it took my mind off...things. For a bit."

"All right." He stepped back. "I'll see you back at the van, then."

"Yeah. And Zeb." Saying his name got him to look right at me, those wide, guileless brown eyes. "Thanks. Not just for this, but for the whole...the whole night, y'know? On stage? That was great."

That got a smile to his damp muzzle. "It was pretty good, wasn't it?"

"Took my mind off things." I touched my nose to his one last time, smelled my own jizz and saliva. "All right. Give me like five or ten minutes and I promise the hall will be clear by then."

"Jackson." I turned at the door and looked back at him. He flicked his ears and then brought them upright. "Thanks for doing this."

"Ah." I waved a paw. "I'm the one who fucked up the night. Might as well do what I can to save it for one of us."

The breeze in the parking lot blew refreshingly around my ears and muzzle, a little cooler than in the stuffy club, especially that closet, though I hadn't minded so much while I was there with Zeb.

The kit fox...what to make of him? There still wasn't a long-term possibility there, not for me, and I was pretty sure not for him either, but that didn't mean we couldn't have a really close friendship. For the duration of the tour, if not beyond.

Matt was leaning against the van, but with his black fur in the shadows, I didn't really notice him until I'd gotten a little closer and the shine of his eyes gleamed as he looked up. I raised a paw. "You didn't have to wait up for me, honey."

He rolled his eyes. "Lars is sleeping. I wanted to talk to you."

I heaved a sigh. All the feelings, the phone call I'd blocked out of my head, Jazmyn having a family with some other guy, the divorce, all came back in a rush, like falling from the top of the world to the bottom in a few seconds. "Sorry about fucking up the songs. I'll tell Lars it was my fault."

"Oh, I already told him that. Didn't matter. I mean, he blames you, but he also said the crowd was shitty, and what else did we expect playing in shitty places like this, and that led into a whole thing…" He waved his paw. "Anyway, we can talk about that. The point is, this East Coast trip has to go well for us to get to those kinds of places, and if you need to take some time off, I can re-book us—maybe."

"Maybe?"

He bobbed his head back and forth. "It might blow up, but I'd rather try than risk showing up when we're not ready."

I took a breath. "I can be ready."

"You sure? We've got two days until the next one, but we have to spend most of one day in the van."

"So?"

"So if you're going to be bringing down the mood…" He let that one just hang there.

"I'm sorry. I'll tell my next wife to time her Dear-Jackson call for when we're not on tour."

"Hey." He held up his paws. "I'm not blaming you. I'm just asking you if you need to take a break from the band."

I breathed the cool air. "No. No, I'll be fine, I promise."

His eyes searched mine. "All right," he said. "But if we have one more fuck-up at a show—"

"I'm sorry!" My heart tightened up again; just the threat of something dire happening if I fucked up again brought me back to divorce, and Jesus Dog, I could not lose Jaz and the band in the same week. "Listen, I understand you're Manager Matt now, but I really need Friend Matt too."

He scowled, and waved me toward the front seat. "Go get some rest. I'll wait for Zeb."

I climbed into the front seat and tucked my tail around my hips like always, and closed my eyes. But I didn't sleep. I thought about Jazmyn and all that was lost to me now, and it hurt like a knife in my gut. The pain hunched me over, but I knew I had to feel it. Bottling it up would leave me like my mom, bitter for years over my dad's abandonment. I didn't feel bitter now and I didn't want this hurt feelings to sour into bitterness. I still loved Jaz and she didn't deserve that.

My ear, close to the closed window, caught the click of claws on the parking lot asphalt. I pressed fingers to my eyes and tried to look asleep in case someone peeked in.

Matt and Zeb talked shortly. Zeb said he'd gone for a walk, and Matt accepted it. A few minutes later, the kit fox opened the side door, and he and Matt climbed in. Matt crawled back to sleep with Lars, and Zeb took his customary passenger side rear seat.

I waited for him to reach out and touch me, but he didn't. Maybe he thought I was already asleep. But the touch would've been really nice.

Day 17: Bittersweet Me

Matt shook me awake sometime annoyingly close to sunrise and offered to drive, but I told him I was in the driver's seat, I'd drive the damn van. We hit a donut shop for breakfast and coffee and then got on the road.

Zeb stayed back in the rear seat, keeping to himself. I'd kinda hoped he'd come up and we could at least smile at each other, but hell, if he wanted some alone time, that was his right. Lars wasn't talking either, and Matt was on his phone typing out some e-mails, so I basically had to sit up and try to keep from thinking about Jazmyn.

The hardest part was knowing that all this was going on while I was hundreds of miles away. She was back home packing my stuff, screwing this other guy, going to the doctor for checkups on the pup, and not only couldn't I be part of it, I couldn't even call to ask her how it was going. I didn't have it to look forward to when I got back. All I had to look forward to was finding a place to stay. Thinking about the various neighborhoods and how much I hated all of them was where I was when Matt clambered his way up through the seats to sit next to me.

"Hey," I said. "Can I crash on your floor for a while when we get back?"

"We have a couch," he said, "but if you'd rather sleep on the floor, you're welcome to."

"Couch, floor, whatever. Thanks."

He nodded. "How you doing?"

"I'm fine. I mean, you know." I gave him a toothy smile. "I'm a coyote. We get kicked down, beat up, shit on. That's just what we call 'life.'"

"Yeah, and being a drama queen is how you deal with it." He acknowledged my smile with a weak one of his own. "All right. Hey, so what happened when we left? The manager said you guys played another fifteen?"

I gave him a short account of what we'd played, leaving out the specifics of the songs. In the mirror, I saw Zeb's ears perk as I mentioned how well we'd played together, but he didn't say anything. "Thanks for pulling it out," Matt said.

"Considering it was my fault in the first place, it's the least I could do."

"So would you consider maybe doing a couple instrumentals as a break in the middle of our set? Give Lars and me a break?"

I side-eyed him. "If you guys are planning on a quickie in the middle of a show, I highly approve of that, but I want you to do it just offstage so I can watch."

"Just taking a break," Matt said, but he glanced back and then lowered his voice. "Lars would never go for it."

"How about we leave him and Zeb on for a number and you can blow me again?" I'd kept my voice low, but I realized after I said it that I hadn't told Zeb, and I didn't want him to find out that way…but the music and road were loud, and he was leaning against the window staring out at it, not reacting at all.

Matt coughed. "Don't go thinking that's going to be a common thing."

"Nah, I know. I mean, in case I meet a stripper on the road and…" I had this whole thing planned where I was going to say that if I married her while on the road and then she divorced me later in the tour, I could hit up Matt for another blow job, but I only got halfway through the first sentence before my chest choked up.

"And?" He knew me well enough to give me the concerned look.

"Then I wouldn't need a blow job from you, obviously." I forced the words out and stared at the road signs. Shippy's Roadside Diner. Exit 255 for Middleton. I-80. I thought about how all the roads had numbers and an order and a place where they all were supposed to be. That distracted me until Matt spoke again, this time to ask if I wanted anything to drink from the cooler, since my coffee was cold.

"I like stanky cold donut shop coffee," I said. "But if you've got some generic store brand sickeningly sweet cherry cola flavored beverage back there, I'd take one."

"I think I can dig that up." He clambered back.

I looked again in the mirror at Zeb, but the kit fox still wasn't paying attention. His muzzle rested against the window glass and his eyes were focused on something out there, or maybe on nothing out there. "Hey," I called back, but he didn't respond.

Okay. I'd let him brood, and I'd talk to him that evening.

But right around the time we were finishing up dinner, with Lars finally showing signs of life, Jazmyn called Matt's phone to talk to me. This time she wanted to fax me some papers I was going to have to sign. "If you want to get a lawyer to look over them, I'll understand, but I'm not trying to rip you off," she said. "I got these off Legaldocs.com and had an…old friend look over them."

I tried to remember the name of that leopard lawyer she'd slept with a few times, and couldn't. "Why are you faxing them?" I asked. "Who even has a fax machine?"

She sighed. "Don't make this harder than it has to be."

"I'm not the one using archaic technology." She didn't say anything. "Fine. Fine. I'll go find a fax machine somewhere. What's his name?"

"What?"

I'd slipped it in there casually, hoping she would just answer before she realized what she was doing. "Nothing."

"Do you really want to know?"

I was leaning against the van while the other three guys were in the restaurant finishing up, the metal door warm from the sun against my back. My tail swished restlessly against it. "I'm going to find out eventually, right? I mean, when people ask 'what happened to your marriage?' I can't just say, 'my wife left me for this other guy, I don't know what his name is, but I guess he was better in bed than me.'"

"Jackson."

"It'd be much easier just to say, 'she left me for this guy Tony,' and then they would think, 'oh, Tony must be better in bed,' but nobody would have to say it."

"*Jackson.*"

"I mean, also, if his name is something like Rudolfo, I could say, 'she left me for a guy named Rudolfo, can you believe it?' and everyone would say, 'is that still a real name?' I mean, they'd still be thinking he was better in bed—"

"He's not."

My ears perked up. "What?"

"He's not better in bed."

"Oh."

"Does that make you happy? Is that what you want to hear?"

I watched clouds drift across the sun. The brightness hurt my eyes. "I dunno. Is it true?"

"Does it matter?"

"Jesus, I hate playing the question game with you. What's his goddamn name?"

She exhaled. "It's Gerald, okay? And look, he was here and you weren't. It was just timing, that's all."

"Sure it was. He's at least better at one thing than I am, huh?"

Her voice wavered. "I didn't mean for that to happen."

"I meant earning money," I lied. "He's in real estate, you said? Is he filthy rich?"

The lie helped her recover her poise. "I'm not doing this right now. Call me when you have a fax number."

I shifted the phone next to my ear. "Why such a hurry?"

"Because we want to get married before the cub's born, and I want time to plan. I'm sorry. It's—it's better that we make a clean break." She took a breath. "It's better for you, too. You can just move on."

"I don't want to move on." That was a lie too, probably, maybe, at least ten percent, but it was an effective one because it made her feel bad, and even if I wouldn't ever take her back (yes I would), I wouldn't have to act on that promise because she wasn't going to take me back. So it was safe, and mean, and that's how she took it.

"I'm sorry. Good-bye."

"Hey!" I yelled, so loudly that a female raccoon stopped to stare at me from the sidewalk. The phone was already dead, so I pointed to it. "Not you," I said. "My wife. She's leaving me for Gerald."

The raccoon frowned at me and then kept walking. "Sorry," I said, shoving the phone in my pocket. "I thought that would sound better out loud than in my head."

The worst part of it was—well, the worst part was losing my family. But as that was wearing off, I was realizing that I didn't have a plan. In the short term, I could crash with Matt, but what was I going to *do*? Back when I was with Jazmyn, I believed there would be cubs one day, that I would settle down and be a father, and maybe the band would work out and maybe it wouldn't, but if it didn't, something else would come along. I'd always be a step ahead of life like a good coyote should be.

And now? Now life had broadsided me, leaving me with a band which, let's be honest, was not going to propel me to stardom or even a regular income unless someone saw me playing guitar and recruited me for another band, and the most physical relationships I was left with now were with my committed best friend and an ex-Mormon who was trying to figure out if he was gay or not. Which was pleasurable and all, but more complicated than I wanted it to be considering there wasn't an endgame there for me.

Zeb came around the corner of the van, saw me, and stopped. I kept staring straight ahead because I wasn't sure if I wanted to talk to him, and I wanted to give him an out in case he wasn't ready to talk to me. He did back away, leaving just his nose and one of his paws showing in my peripheral vision.

I drummed my fingers against the side of the van, now thinking about Zeb as a nice distraction from the rest of my life. Why was he being all twitchy around me? Uncertain about the blow job he'd given, or the one he'd been promised and hadn't received? Or had he sensed there was something wrong from the phone call and didn't want to disturb me? I'd heard all sorts of things about the politeness of Mormons (that'd be a good band name, wouldn't it?), so I couldn't rule that out.

I was about halfway there when Zeb came back around the corner of the van, clearing his throat. "Ah…hey, Jackson."

"Hi." I raised a paw. "You guys ready to get on the road?"

"Just about." He leaned against the van a little ways away from me. "You doing okay?"

"Yeah. I need to find a fax machine."

"Oh." He pulled out his phone. "So like a FedEx store?"

I scanned the street in front of us. There were a lot of old storefronts, a couple convenience stores, a gas station, and a sandwich place. Broken glass glittered in the gutters and an issue of the local free paper, separated into its component pages, fluttered around in the breeze. "Is that a thing that exists in this town?"

That got a chuckle out of him, which notched my mood upward one tick. "There's got to be one. Did you ask at the gas station?"

"I hadn't gotten that far yet." My question about why he was so twitchy surfaced, and I pushed it back down. "Hey, can I ask you something?"

His ears went down and when he said, "Yeah," it was a little guarded.

"What do you think the ceiling is for the band?"

He blinked and his ears came back up. "This band? REMake?" I nodded. "Uh…" He put a paw to his muzzle. "Well, if there's an R.E.M. tribute album in a couple years, we might get asked to do a cover."

I had to laugh. "So you don't see sold out stadium tours, platinum records…"

Now he looked like he was trying to figure out if I were insane. "For a cover band? Um…"

"Relax. I don't either." I sighed.

"Well…" His tail brushed the van, back and forth. "What do you see?"

"We get to go around the country and play music and hang out, and we make enough for new instruments. Maybe someone sees us and calls R.E.M. and like one of the guys comes to see us play and likes our arrangements. That's the ceiling for me."

He tilted his muzzle. "You pretty much told me that at the start of the tour. I mean, you said Matt thought there was a path to…"

I picked up where he'd left off. "Yeah, I know, Matt and his 'new music landscape.' I just can't see it. I mean, you'd hear about shit like that, right? 'U2 Cover Band Selected To Play UFL Championship Halftime' or something?"

His ears stayed cupped toward me. "Are you okay, Jackson?"

"I'm fine. I'm just wondering…is this worth it?"

He didn't give me the falsely reassuring immediate "yes," but considered the question as though there were lots of angles to it, as though the answer weren't blindingly obvious. "For me, it's a lot of good practice playing melodic songs I really like. I can study them and it helps me when I go to write my own stuff." When I didn't say anything, he nudged me. "You should write more music. That song you wrote is really good."

I pressed my head back against the van and closed my eyes. "I need some other…inspiration to write, then."

That remark fell into a dead silence. I watched a lemur shuffle out of the liquor store with a brown paper bag. He stopped, looked blearily our way, and then lifted the mouth of the bag to his muzzle.

"Uh, the other guys will be here soon," Zeb said finally. He pushed himself away from the van and laid a quick paw on my shoulder, gone almost as soon as I noticed it. "Hope you feel better," he said.

He started to walk away and I called after him, "Hey, Zeb?"

His ears folded down. What was his problem? "Yeah?" he said without turning.

"What inspires you?"

He stopped, and his ears came up. "What do you mean?"

"To write music. To keep going, doing this." I gestured back at the van.

One of his paws reached out to touch the side of the van, and his tail swished as he turned. "Oh, gosh," he said. "It's music. I mean, how can you not keep doing it?"

I nodded and looked down at my paws. "Maybe when your life falls apart, you'll know."

Again, he looked awkward, and said, "I'm really sorry about that."

"It'd be a hell of a lot harder without you guys and this tour, you know?" I took a breath and started to tell him that I appreciated his company, but just then both our ears perked up at the sound of Lars and Matt approaching.

"I know Matt's one of your best friends," Zeb said in a low voice.

I smiled. "You've all been good."

And then Matt and Lars were there and I told them I needed to find a FedEx. Lars said, "Need to make extra copies of your sheet music?" and I said it was nice to see that our lead singer had a voice again, and Matt told us both to shut up, but it was nice to get back to the collegial poking at each other, and nobody's tail was down as we got back into the van.

We found a 24-hour FedEx office about twenty minutes away, and I used their desk phone to call Jazmyn. A few minutes later, the purple-shirted possum pushed eighteen pages across the counter. "How much?" I asked.

"Sender paid," he said. "For the reply, too."

"Reply?" Matt was waiting with me; Zeb and Lars were in the van. It had occurred to me that this was kind of the solution to a logic puzzle: what configuration of two parties can you split the band into to be sure that nobody's having sex? Then I remembered Matt blowing me a few days ago.

"What?" I realized he was still talking.

"Does she expect you to read this entire thing and send it back in an hour or something?"

"Oh."

The possum leaned forward. "You can just bring it back tomorrow or the next day or whatever."

"We have to be in Peco tomorrow," Matt told him. "Can we take it to a FedEx there?"

"Uh." He scratched behind his head. "Which one?"

"I'll just sign it," I said.

Matt raised a paw to the possum. "We'll just be a second." He grabbed me and pulled me over to the self-copying section.

"Ugh," I said. "Can we assume I've heard the whole 'don't sign anything you haven't read' speech, and you've heard the whole 'I trust Jazmyn and I just want to be done with this' speech and let me go back and sign it?"

"You trust Jazmyn," Matt said. "But do you trust the guy she's leaving you for? Do you trust the lawyer she hired to draw this up?"

I sighed and shook the papers at him. "What are they going to do? We rent, everything I want to own is basically this body," I gestured to myself, "and the guitar I have in the van, and I barely have any money in savings."

"Just read it. We've got a whole day tomorrow." He tried to take the papers, but I held them away from him.

"Yeah, that's my idea of a fun day. Sitting in the van reading divorce papers. Hey, why don't I drive and you read them aloud to me? That sound like fun?"

He raised his eyebrows. The tips of his fangs showed over his dead serious expression. "I'll do it if you want."

"You know," I said, settling a paw on his shoulder, "as much as I love to call your bluffs, I think that's a little too much misery to share. Not that I mind you having to read the legalese about the dissolution of my relationship, but think of the children. No, I think I'll just sign it and fax it back."

Matt shook his head. "As your friend, Jackson, I can't let you do that."

"You," I removed the paw from his shoulder, "don't get a say."

"Well," he said as I stepped toward the counter, "do you still want to crash at my place when we're done the tour?"

My ears flattened and my tail curled down. Fuck. "Seriously? You're holding me hostage?"

"I prefer to think of it as being your conscience with a little more leverage." When I looked back at him, he had a self-satisfied smile that went the whole length of his muzzle.

"Fucking hell," I said, loudly enough to draw a disapproving glare from the marten making copies of his multi-volume novel or something, to judge by the stacks of paper surrounding him like a cub's play fort. "Fine. And by the way, leave the smirking to the coyotes and foxes who can actually pull it off."

So I stalked back to the counter and we got the address of a FedEx in Peco. I curled up the divorce papers in my paw and held them like a club as we walked back out to the van.

Day 18: Bad Day

I spent the next day huddled up in the passenger seat behind Matt as he drove pushing my brain through "The court in the parties' dissolution action shall reserve jurisdiction" and "If either party has incurred or does incur, on or before the effective date of this agreement, any liability not disclosed and listed in this agreement on which the other is or may become personally liable or that could be enforced at any time against an asset held or to be received…" and on and on, eighteen pages' worth, including the cover page and the letter from the lawyer, whose name was, I shit you not, Alvertino Principio (I was pretty sure it was the leopard guy, because I vaguely remembered making fun of that name at the time) explaining that all of this was boilerplate really and that he'd made very few alterations to it, all at Jazmyn's request. He hadn't done a very thorough job of it; I found a bunch of little things like splitting up the home equity we didn't have, and a reference to a prenup we didn't have, and other parts I skimmed rather than read because my heart tightened and refused to beat just from looking at the section titles.

The cause for divorce was listed as "spousal infidelity," and I thought, hoo boy, if they only knew. I snuck a glance over at Zeb, but he wasn't looking at me, just noodling around on his bass guitar, notes I could barely hear over the engine noise. In front of him, Lars did some vocal exercises when he wasn't talking to Matt.

Round about page thirteen, it sunk in that this was basically all the life I had left. And when the tour was over, then what? I'd be crashing with Matt and Lars until I could find my own place, I'd continue to do contract work for the construction crew to make ends meet, and wait for the next tour. If it happened.

If I wanted a family, I'd have to start from scratch. At 25-almost-26, that wasn't the end of the world, but it was disheartening. I'd put three years into the relationship with Jazmyn, with nothing to show for it. I didn't even know where to go to meet another coyote girl, unless I went back to the strip clubs.

"It looks fine," I said to Matt when we stopped at the FedEx in Peco. "Just like I knew it would."

"We had the time." He held the door and followed me in.

"I could've been practicing on my guitar. You know I need practice, right? But hey, at least it kept me from whipping my cock out on the drive here, right?"

He flattened his ears, and the cacomistle behind the counter paused with his paw on the contract. "Uh, so, you guys need me to fax this?"

"Please," Matt said to him, "and I'm sorry for my friend. He's going through a divorce."

Whether the cacomistle—Jordy, according to his name tag—cared about that or not I couldn't tell. He just took the pages and went to the back.

"You know that's not what this was about," Matt said in a low voice, keeping it fairly steady, to his credit.

I shrugged. "Whatever."

"I have been looking out for you throughout this marriage." He started to get his older brother voice on.

"So what do you want? You want me to bow down and say you were right, I shouldn't have married her?"

"No. I'm just telling you that's over now. Next time you fuck a girl in the bathroom and decide to marry her, I'll just keep my mouth shut. And when she divorces you and you just sign the agreement, I'll—well, to be honest I'll probably be somewhere else. Making music."

"You think I won't be making music?"

He started to say something, then closed his mouth and shook his head. "I'm not gonna get into this."

"No, please." Jordy was making a lot of beeps back at the fax machine. "Get into it. What, I'm going to give up the band for family? I'm here, ain't I?"

"Exactly." He stabbed at my chest with a finger. "You want it all, family and band and music and whatever, and as a result you're getting divorced, you're half-assing it with the band—I know, I know, you play great. You could be better, though."

"I'll have plenty of time now." I kept my voice stone cold.

"Until the next strip club bathroom."

"At least I know I'll always have you around to remind me what I could be doing better with my life."

His ears went down, matching mine, and we both looked away from each other, me aware that he was just trying to help, and him aware that he was being an ass. I think, anyway. My mind skittered off to wish that Jaz had come on the tour with us and thinking about how awkward that would've been, and then Matt cleared his throat, his voice back to normal.

"Hey," he said. "Let's find a place to jam tonight."

I raised an eyebrow and an ear. "Don't we need to practice?"

"Hell yes." He snorted. "But we can have fun, too. That's sort of like practice."

"Fine." To be honest, I wasn't up for jamming, but I'd been kind of a dick with the cock comment, pun intended, and Matt was trying to do something nice, so I figured I'd let him.

Jordy came back and said the sender's account number had been corrupted on the fax and his best guess hadn't worked, so he charged us twenty-three bucks to send the contract. Matt insisted on paying for it even though I told him it made me feel shitty for someone else to be paying for my divorce, and he said, "We're *all* paying for it."

My ears went back and I felt shitty all over again, like not only was I having to go through this, but I was putting my friends through it, too. Well, fuck him. I fake-laughed and said to Jordy, "He blew me the other night, you know."

The black wolf made a strangled noise, and Jordy did his best impression of a deaf cacomistle. "That's not why I'm getting divorced," I assured him. "My wife got pregnant with some other guy. Gerald. So obviously..." I waved a paw.

Matt kept staring at me. "You know what?" he said finally. "Pay for your own goddamn divorce." And he turned and stalked out of the store.

Jordy looked down at the counter. The air conditioner hummed in the background and one of the machines in back made a beeping noise. I looked at the rack of candy for sale, trying to figure out how I was going to pay for this, and after a long silence, Jordy spoke. "So, uh," he said. "Twenty-three dollars."

"Okay," I said, "the thing is, I don't actually have any money on me. My credit card's in the van."

It was my credit card, but Jaz had told me to be careful with the purchases, not that that mattered now anyway. Would she pay the bill when it arrived? Zeb might have fronted me the money, but I didn't really want to ask him and anyway, I didn't know his phone number.

"Well..." Jordy said, "it's twenty-three dollars."

"I know. Hang on." I could go out and get Matt, but I didn't want to go begging to him. I didn't have anyone else to call... "Okay, what if I call my ex-wife and get the account number that's supposed to be on it?"

"Sure." Jordy nodded, and kept looking at me. The waiting stretched on until I realized he wasn't going to offer.

I cleared my throat. "Um. Can I borrow a phone?"

When Jazmyn picked up, she was cautious. "What is it?"

"I just need the account number for the fax. They can't find it or it's smeared or something. I signed the papers, don't worry about that. I would've paid for it myself, but—"

"Don't worry about it," she said. "Put the FedEx guy on."

So she gave the account info to Jordy and settled it while I stewed about what she'd said. *Don't worry about it.* Twenty-three dollars was a week's food budget for us once upon a time. What she was telling me was that Gerald had a lot of money, that he was a better provider than me, that he was a better everything than me.

"All set," Jordy said. He gave me a receipt and I crumpled it and threw it at the trash. It bounced off the edge and onto the floor, and I walked outside.

Matt was waiting for me at the van, the others probably inside. "You didn't say she was pregnant, before."

"I know."

He sighed and rested a paw on my arm. I thought he was going to say something like, "This is the danger of an open relationship," and then I was going to have to tell him to lay off, and I was on edge and kinda wanted him to say that.

But he didn't. "I'm sorry," he said, and hugged me. And that was almost worse because it made me cry. Just a little, and I think I covered it up, but probably not well enough. For a moment, the hollow feeling I'd had all day ebbed and I was feeling feelings again.

"I shouldn't have walked out," he said, but I cut him off before he could say anything else.

"Don't worry about it," I said, and climbed into the van, the hollow feeling already coming back.

Night 18: Fall On Me

That night, we found a park where a couple other musicians were playing, set up in a spot away from them, and jammed for about an hour until a cop came up and told us to pack up. "I'm being nice on account of I like the music," he said, "but you can't play in public without a permit."

The other musicians had melted away or else been warned off while we hadn't noticed. So we packed up our things and grabbed some food at a nearby diner.

"Hey," I said as we were wrapping up, "Matt, you and Lars want the van for a bit? It's been a while, I know."

"Oh," Matt said, and looked at Lars, who gave a firm nod. "I guess so."

"Thanks," Lars said. "It *has* been a while."

I waved a paw in the sign of a cross. "Let it not be said that Jackson Alley is blind to the needs of others. Especially good friends. Now go forth and fuck well."

"Uh-huh." Lars gave me a side-eye, but smiled as he did it. I checked out Zeb's reaction, but he was pretty much buried in the remnants of his fries.

So once Lars and Matt took off, I asked the waitress for recommendations for a good dessert place, and she said, "Hon, we got a cheesecake here will put two pounds on you just when you look at it."

"We've got room," I said. "Any other desserts?"

"Sure. You can have it plain or with strawberry topping."

"Is that fresh strawberries or the gooey pie filling kind of topping?"

She was a lively, sassy ferret, and she gave me a look and a smirk. "It's the gooey topping. What, you think a place with Miller Lite signs on the walls has fresh strawberries?"

"Zeb, how's that sound to you?"

The kit fox looked up. "Okay, I guess," he said.

"One with strawberry goo and one without," I told the waitress.

"Coming right up," she said, and headed back to the kitchen.

Zeb was still not looking at me, still sitting there with his paws folded on the table, his ears so flat you could sit a drink on 'em. "Hey," I said, and he looked up guiltily, like I'd caught him thinking about me. "Look, I'm not gonna bite you. Just want to talk a bit, okay?"

"Yeah…" He nodded and flicked his eyes away, then back.

I sighed and leaned a little closer. "You've just been all quiet ever since…that night, y'know? I didn't think it was that bad, but something's bothering ya. Was it getting it on your face? That's kind of an advanced move, I'll admit. Most guys don't like to clean it out of their fur."

"Sort of," he said, and I could see the tension ease out of his shoulders. "It was just weird."

"Not weird good, I'm gonna guess?"

"Ugh." He leaned forward, nose almost to the table, and linked his paws behind his head. "It wasn't you. I mean, I li—I liked it when you…I liked giving that to you."

"I liked getting it." I reached out, then drew my paw back. I didn't know if he wanted to be touched. "So…?"

He took a breath, and when he spoke, his voice was very small. "All the stuff I was taught, all the things I'm trying to get rid of, it all came back. I literally heard my Elder yelling at me that I was foul and I was staring in the mirror and it was dripping off my fur…"

I did put a paw on his arm then, and though he jerked at the touch, he didn't pull away from it. "I don't want to push you into anything," I said. "We don't have to do that ever again if you don't want to. I just don't want to fuck up the band and—"

I didn't get to the heartfelt, sensitive part of my speech, because he snapped his head around. "That's not the problem," he said. "I do want to do it again, that's the problem. I liked how it felt in my mouth and I liked what it did to you, but I'm afraid of getting that voice again telling me how terrible I am."

"Ah, jeez." What the hell do you say to that? *Sorry your religion fucked you up?* Compared to him, my troubles didn't seem so bad. Yeah, I had no family, no real prospects for a future, but at least I didn't have a voice inside me telling me I was going to burn in hell for the things I was wired for. And I wasn't sure I could even offer him comfort. If my God had appeared to me in a flaming tree or something and said, "THOU SHALT NOT SUCK COCK," I would probably be okay with it. I mean, I'd feel guilty about not giving backsies when Zeb or Matt did it (less so with Matt because he had Lars). I was still determined to get my muzzle around Zeb's cock before the end of the tour—or, if that would upset him too much, figure out the equivalent. Jackson Alley pays his debts.

Zeb turned an eye toward me, peering under his arm. "What would you do?"

"You don't want to take my advice." The words just spilled out the way they do sometimes. "I got my sermons from the church of Life. Mom and Dad weren't churchy people and I just learned to be good to other people and don't take what ain't yours. So I guess I'd just go ahead and do what I wanted to do as long as I was sure it wasn't going to hurt anyone."

"You don't believe in an immortal soul?"

I shrugged. "That's a heavy question. But I mean, what does it matter if I believe in it or not? If it exists, it exists. Either way you should make it happy."

That was right around when the waitress came back with the cheesecake. She held the two plates and said, "Okay, I'm guessing the smart mouth gets the goo?"

"I hope so," I said, and Zeb's eyes widened. He unlinked his paws and sat up, and the waitress dropped the strawberry-syrup-coated cheesecake in front of me and the plain one in front of Zeb. Two forks clattered down to follow.

"Enjoy, boys," she said, and sashayed away. My eye followed her rear and the cute black-tipped tail swinging across it, and I thought, if I flirted a bit more, I could hit that. My sheath approved of that thought, but I reminded myself that Zeb was here and that we had other problems to address.

It did give me an idea, though. "Hey," I said. "Would you feel better if I set you up with a girl?"

"Huh?" He was teasing the tines of the fork around the top of the cheesecake.

"Like our waitress. You think she was cute?"

His ears flopped to the side. "I guess?"

"You didn't notice her?"

He set his fork down. "She took our order. She's a ferret. Her name is...uh..." I didn't help him. "Roselie?"

"Close. Jill."

He shook his head. "How did you know that?"

I steepled my eyebrows. "I deduced it, Watson, through the simple expedient of reading it off her nametag."

He snorted and turned his attention back to the cheesecake, taking a bite. "I don't notice girls really."

"All right." I speared the tip of my cheesecake. It dripped red as I brought it to my muzzle. "I was just thinking I could help with something that didn't bother your inner childhood so much."

"I know." He sighed and took another bite. "I've just got to get over it. This is really good, by the way."

"The goo isn't bad, but I think it's out of a can." The cake was excellent, though, creamy and fluffy with just a hint of sourness. "Okay, I'll leave you alone about it, I guess, unless there's something else I can do."

"Thanks." He spoke in a low voice. "I'm sorry for being weird about it."

"Don't apologize. I kinda want to go punch your Elder, though."

His eyes widened in horror. "Oh, no! Don't do that!"

"Settle down." I grinned and licked strawberry from my lips. "I don't even know where he lives, and I wouldn't punch him. Far too direct for a coyote."

"Don't do anything to him." Zeb stared at me.

"Fine, fine." I waggled my eyebrows. "I'll focus on undoing his work on you. All with your permission and participation, of course."

"Mmm." He filled his mouth with cheesecake and then, as though he'd been gathering his courage to do it, stuck his tongue out at me with cheesecake all over it.

I took that as a good sign, and also a sign that we'd done about as much as we were going to do on that road tonight. "Okay, how about we talk about me for a bit?"

"What?" He remembered as he said that. "Oh, gosh, Jackson, I'm sorry."

"Don't apologize." I licked strawberry off my fork. "I think I figured out what I want to do, but I don't know how."

"What?"

It was my turn to hesitate, because from the time I got into music, it was always just a hobby, just a way to pass the time, nothing serious, like the way some guys golf and some guys fish. I'd promised Jazmyn that.

(And then I disappeared on tours for weeks on end.)

So I took a breath and said, "I want to really do something with music."

He brightened, and I wondered what he thought I'd been thinking of saying, or if he'd just been dreading yet another maundering ramble from Jackson about the betrayals in his life. "Like writing songs?"

"Uh-huh." I started the next bit in my head and then had to reword it; I didn't want to tell him that the best I'd felt was jamming with him, because I didn't want him to think it was about him. "You were encouraging me to do that, and I realized that playing my song, the thing I wrote, in front of all those people, even though most of them didn't give a shit…that was fun. It was just hard to see that because…well, you know."

"Yeah." He flicked his ears, but they didn't stay down this time. "It's a good song. And the people did like it. I mean, the ones that were still paying attention."

I tossed my muzzle. "Part of this too is that I don't just want to play for a bunch of drunk yahoos in bars."

"Um." He took another bite of cheesecake and waved his fork at me. "You might want to take a look at Matt's schedule for the next two weeks, then."

"Oh, I'll finish the tour. I still love the band, and Matt and Lars are great guys. Matt says I can stay with him after the tour until I get on my feet again. But afterwards…I want to do something more serious."

I filled my muzzle with cake again and watched Zeb. I could see him struggling to decide whether he should offer to write with me, and saw the *not yet* pass over his muzzle. He just nodded and said, "Cool."

After dessert, I suggested we give Matt and Lars a little more time and take a stroll through the neighborhood. "Is it safe?" Zeb asked, and I told him I thought a coyote and kit fox could probably defend themselves pretty well, even if we were just scrawny musicians. That didn't make him feel better, so I said we'd stick to well-lit main roads, and then he agreed to come along.

The town we were in, or the section of Peco, felt cramped and old in a way you don't get out on the Left Coast, even at the island of neon and cars in the middle of a five-way intersection where the diner lived. I chose the largest road and the direction that showed the most life: storefront lights over metal grates, windows of dusty electronics with hand-lettered prices, a neon red and blue "Bail Bonds" sign and a simple hanging sign that read "COIN WASH" advertising the only two other businesses that seemed to be open at this time of night as we walked past them.

Amid those stores rose tall apartment buildings, red brick with a checkerboard-straight pattern of windows in each one and "First Month Rent $200" or big loud phone numbers hanging on each. Down side streets, row houses stretched as far as we could see, ten or twenty or fifty different houses all squeezed together to cram into one street. We passed a few people, and the stream of cars remained light but steady; nobody really bothered us.

At the end of the street, just around the convenience store on the corner out front of which three cougars sat smoking, we found a little park bounded only by tall hedges, overseen by a dark metal statue of some horse in uniform holding a sword. A few lights illuminated empty park benches through a light humid haze, and in the darker areas, the glow of cigarette ends explained the smoke that prickled at my nose.

"Let's sit for a bit," Zeb said, surprising me. He led me to a bench that our eyes picked out of the dim light, away from the streetlamps.

I sat on the cold wood and he sat next to me. "Don't want to stay in the light?"

"We can see or hear anyone coming," he said. "I just want to sit in the quiet for a bit."

"Okay." It wasn't a bad idea. The peace of the park felt nice, even with the smoke, and the late summer air had lost its heat, if not the humidity.

For a couple minutes, we just sat, and I was happy enough that I could just zone out and let my mind go blank. Then Zeb said softly, "Can you hear the music more clearly at times like this?"

I hadn't really thought about that, to be honest. Music just came to me, or more often didn't, so there wasn't really enough experience for me to tell that it happened better in such-and-such circumstance or other. So I leaned back and tried to tune out the low constant growl of engines behind us, watched Zeb with his ears up and mimicked his posture, and listened.

For a bit, nothing happened. And then I heard Jazmyn's song in my head, felt the guitar strings. My paws twitched, fingers sliding and plucking imaginary strings, and in the silence, my mind wandered, exploring the melody, letting it carry me away.

"Jackson?"

I blinked back into the kit fox's eyes. "Hm?"

"Oh. I thought you might've fallen asleep. You didn't say anything."

"I was listening to the music. Like you said."

"Sorry!" He swung those big ears back and ducked his head abashedly.

Across from us, the glow of a cigarette flared and then dropped to the ground. Footsteps shuffled across the dirt of the park, carrying a pair of lynxes into the glow of a light and then dropping them back into shadow, just two silhouettes and the receding noise of their departure. A whiff of pot smoke trailed after them, then dissipated, but their footsteps remained as a beat in my head. "Don't be sorry," I said in a low voice. "I haven't done original compositions a whole lot. I'm learning how to do it."

"Me too." He replied in the same hushed voice, sliding closer to me on the bench. His tail flipped over mine. "You get anything good?"

"I was going back to Jazmyn's song."

"Oh."

He looked sad for me, so I leaned in and nuzzled him. "Don't be sad. I still like the song, and you know, I loved her. That's real, that doesn't vanish just because we're not together now. I'm just trying to reimagine the song as a tribute to a memory rather than a, y'know, a love song."

"Plenty of good love songs like that," he said, and his breath smelled of cheesecake, and I knew I was going to kiss him only a second before I did it.

I think he knew it too, because he didn't act surprised at all. His lips met mine and his arm slid around my side. The music in my head changed and danced, and I pulled him closer.

We kissed in the empty park while the stars spun overheard and the horse soldier watched silently. Then we broke apart and sat, noses touching, and I saw the deep black space between the bushes, behind the bench, and I grinned at him.

"Oh, no," he whispered when I pulled him up and dragged him behind the bench. "Jackson—"

He wasn't resisting, though, and speed mattered, so I yanked him to the ground and then put my nose to his ear. "I just wanted a little more privacy." My paw snuck between his legs, and he drew in a gasp and squirmed. "I'll stop if you want, though."

"But," he protested weakly, "out here…"

He wasn't protesting what I was doing, just where I was doing it. "Shhh. Listen."

We listened. Cars drove by ten feet away, beyond bushes and empty sidewalks. No light penetrated into our little space; even letting my eyes adjust, I could barely make out the softly lit outline of his uncertain smile, the glint of his eyes. Below my paw, his sheath throbbed.

"Nobody's around," I whispered. "I won't let anything happen to you."

The tingle of cigarette smoke reminded us that someone *could* come around. The spice of danger was probably what had Zeb so hard when he let me pull his pants open amid the plant and earth scents of the park. He squeaked softly when my paw grasped him, warm and soft on the outside with a rapidly hardening core underneath. Drops of arousal leaked from his smooth tip as my claws trailed through his fur all around it, down to his balls, along his inner thigh, and though his labored attempts not to make a sound mostly failed, they weren't loud enough for pedestrians passing a few feet from us to hear. The bushes did crunch and crackle as we shifted our weight, but I didn't think that would be enough to alert anyone passing by either.

He closed his eyes, maybe out of passion, maybe to forget where we were; in either case, leaving himself entirely in my paws. And while a couple days ago I'd have gone right ahead, now my confidence had been cracked and bruised. I had my paw there around him again and believe me when I tell you that I wanted to give him an experience he wouldn't soon forget. Jaz and I—nope, better not go to that topic. I just wanted the kid to have fun.

But I also didn't want him to resent me afterwards. Dammit, I was second-guessing myself now. I turned my muzzle to the street and peered through the kaleidoscope of the bushes. Nobody was walking nearby that I could see. The street, too, was empty, though there were sounds of an argument or a party a block away.

All right, Jackson. The longer you dawdle, the longer it'll take.

So I lowered my muzzle to Zeb's and kissed his nose. His eyelids fluttered and he looked up at me. "Hurry," he said softly.

I slid my paw up him again and found him damper than before. So I started a nice, easy rhythm, and I felt the tension in his body where I leaned against him. His paw reached around to my side and his ears flicked back.

It wouldn't be too long, I thought, not the way his tail thrashed against the leaves. I could smell him now, too, a rich foxy musk that rose through the humid night and the chlorophyll smell of the leaves he was breaking. I was excited too, and I leaned in against him, prepared to muffle his muzzle with mine if he started making too much noise.

"Hey! You kids at it again?"

Light flashed past my eyes as we both jerked upright at the loud, authoritative bark. "Shoot," Zeb hissed, and grabbed for his pants, yanking them closed as we both scrambled to our feet.

Behind the accusatory glare of the flashlight, an antlered silhouette stood in front of the horse soldier. "All right, you two, this isn't the seventies," he said. "You've got plenty of places to go, and most will cost less than a two hundred dollar citation. Get your IDs out please."

He lowered the flashlight for a moment, and I grabbed Zeb's paw. "Run!" I said, and yanked him along. By the time he realized what we were doing, I think, we were already out of the park.

The cop ran after us, but we had a bit of a head start and the cop was heavier and older than we were. I turned down a street and then took the next turn at random, not going in any particular direction. The crackle of his radio and his voice followed us, and then even that vanished. When we paused to catch our breath and look back, he wasn't anywhere in sight.

"Darn it," Zeb panted. "Why'd we run?"

"Do you have two hundred dollars? Or want to explain to Matt why we need it?"

"But he was a cop."

"Uh-huh. And we'll be long gone from here tomorrow. He didn't get a good look at us; maybe a sniff, but how will he ever get close enough to smell us again?"

"I've never been in trouble with the cops." He leaned over, paws on his knees, and glared at me.

The fun of running away, the thrill of almost being caught and then of being caught and still getting away with it, all that was evaporating almost as fast as our arousal. "You still aren't," I pointed out. "He's not going to file a report on two guys who were *maybe* doing something he didn't see clearly. First of all, it's not that big a deal. Second of all, he's not going to want to admit that he got outrun. So just chill already."

He straightened and leaned against the brick wall. "Did you have to pick the worst-smelling alley?"

"Hides our scents better in case he's sniffing for them. But he was a deer or elk or something and I'm not sure he'd be able to distinguish our scents."

"There aren't that many kit foxes out here on the East Coast," he pointed out.

"So he probably doesn't even know what one smells like. Come on, just quit…"

I trailed off as we both stared toward the mouth of the alley. Silently, ominously, blue and red flashing lights washed across the bricks where the alley opened onto the main street.

"I hate you," he said.

I grabbed his paw. "Time for that later. Come on."

There was a chance that he was still on foot and had radioed a car to try to herd us toward him. So as we worked our way away from the car,

I kept a sharp lookout for antlers ahead of us. A deer sat with a wolf and bobcat drinking from a brown paper bag, but he didn't have a flashlight and definitely wasn't a cop. None of them paid us any mind as we padded hurriedly past them.

When we came out onto the main street that led back to the diner, both of us stopped to look left and right. No flashing lights in sight, no cop with a flashlight, nothing but scattered pedestrians and there, about a quarter mile away, home.

Regardless, I didn't want to go along this street. If we crossed, went up a block and to the right, maybe we would come to one of the other streets that met the diner. The neighborhood there lay dark and shadowed under trees, a hill beginning to rise away from the apartments into single brick homes with gabled roofs and yards, a quiet area definitely devoid of red and blue flashing lights.

But Zeb said, "Let's just hurry along the street. It's quicker, and we can still see him coming."

"We're still close to the park," I objected. "This is one of the streets he'll cruise down sooner or later, and then we'll either get caught or have to duck out of the way."

"Then go skulk around in the dark," he said. "Maybe we should split up anyway. He's looking for two guys."

It made sense, more sense than what I was proposing. But I didn't want to leave him alone, and I said so.

"I can look after myself," he said, his ears flat back.

"I told you I'd take care of you." I paused until he looked at me, which took a long time. "Hey, I'm sorry. I shouldn't have pulled you back there. But I'm not going to abandon you."

His scowl didn't lessen, but at least his ears came up a bit. "Fine," he said. "Follow me. Just walk normally and act casual."

I stifled a giggle as he stepped out onto the street. Here he'd never been in trouble with the police, and yet he was directing me how to walk. It was adorable.

We walked casually, like he wanted (except that he was holding his tail as stiff as his cock had been fifteen minutes ago, but I didn't want to point that out), alongside each other but not touching, until we were a block from the diner. There we waited for the light to change, and up ahead we could see the van, the light on inside so we knew Matt and Lars were finished.

Zeb had relaxed, his tail swishing so that he actually looked as casual as he wanted to be. And then to our right, those blue and red lights came around the corner.

"Oh, no," he moaned, and bolted across the street before I could say anything.

So much for casual. The cop tapped his siren and the "bloop" echoed through the quiet neighborhood. Zeb made for the diner parking lot, and the best course of action here would be for me to take off down the street, the easy target for the cop to follow. He'd leave Zeb and I could lose him up in the wild dark trees.

But I still didn't want to abandon Zeb unless I was sure the cop was going to follow me. Once I saw the kit fox take off for the diner, I ran *at* the cop car.

It sounded the siren's "bloop" again. Then as I got closer, the door opened and the cop, a big tiger, it looked like, peeked out from behind the door and yelled at me to stop. I skidded to a halt, but if I let him take me here, he'd still have time to get Zeb. I had to make sure he'd chase me, and besides, I had a bunch of resentment built up that I could send his way.

So I flipped him off with both paws. Then I turned tail and dashed back the way I'd come.

I gained a precious few seconds because he didn't get back into his car right away; I think he was deciding whether to chase me on foot or not. I wish he had, because he'd never have outrun a coyote. But the car revved up a moment later, and so I went with my original plan and headed up to the darkness.

The problem was, it was a bit farther to the dark part of the street than I'd calculated, or maybe it was just that the car was faster. "Stop running," the cop blared through a roof speaker, loudly enough that now we were drawing attention from people out on the streets.

A few teenagers ahead of me, bobcats or lynxes or something, turned and cheered me on. "Go, dude!"

As I approached them I yelled, "Where can I hide?"

They fell silent. One of them said, "Go dude!" again as I passed them.

Great. Lots of help. I sped past them and the car pulled up alongside me under a streetlight, the base of the hill and the end of the lights still a good forty yards away. "Stop," the speaker blared again, and I considered my options. The buildings ran pretty continuously to the next intersection, no alleys or narrow passages to duck into. In another

second, the tiger was going to get out of the car and chase me, and if I kept on running, he might tase me or shoot me. And Zeb was safe; at least, I hoped he was. Furthermore, I hadn't really done anything wrong.

So I stopped and stood there as the door opened, and next thing I knew, I was on the ground with a knee in my back and an ache in my muzzle where it had hit the pavement. And that just brought back painful memories of the night I met Jazmyn, which reinforced the fact that I was alone this time. But I did this for Zeb, I reminded myself, and focused on the current situation.

"Fuckin' coyotes." Tiger Cop snapped some cuffs on me and then yanked me to my feet.

What they don't tell you on those cop shows is how the cuffs dig into your wrists, but Jazmyn had warned me about it, so I scrambled quickly to my feet to minmize that, trying to present a dignified, non-intoxicated demeanor. "What seems to be the trouble, officer?" I asked.

Only I didn't quite come off that smooth, because my lip was bleeding from the pavement and starting to swell up, and I couldn't wipe the trickles of blood out of my fur, so I inadvertently sprayed some at him when I talked. Pure accident. Tiger Cop just said, "Get in the car," slapped a paw atop my head between my ears, and forced me into the back seat.

The other thing they don't tell you about on cop shows is how terrible the back seats smell. I swear someone had used it as a toilet very recently, and I classified at least three different species scents, possibly four or five different individuals, and there was also possibly some blood that wasn't mine. "I'm innocent," I said loudly as Tiger Cop slid into the front seat, but with the practiced ear of someone who has ridden with people much more belligerent than me in the back, he ignored me and pulled away (that, now, you do see on cop shows).

"Your friend from the park," he said as we drove past the diner slowly, "he was another coyote?"

"I don't know what you're talking about," I said. "I haven't been in any park tonight."

"Did he go back to the diner?"

"Who?"

He pulled into the narrow lot in front of the diner, at an angle such that I couldn't see the van, and got out without another word. I watched him go into the diner, talk to one of the waitresses and point out at me in the car. I flattened my ears and thought unrecognizable thoughts, looking away at the parking lot and willing Zeb not to come out looking for me like a noble idiot.

He didn't, and when Tiger Cop came back, he got in the car and pulled out. "Waitress in there says there were three coyotes in tonight, one with three guys, one with a female coyote, one by himself. Any of those sound like you?"

I considered. "I did have dinner there with three friends. That might've been me."

He huffed and circled the diner parking lot slowly. *Stay hidden, Zeb,* I thought as hard as I could. *Or be already in the van.*

Nothing moved, and after five minutes of this torture, the cop pulled away. "All right," he said. "I guess you can tell your story at the station."

"It's a boring story," I said, having been working on it some. "I'm afraid it does involve a slight amount of intoxicant."

He snorted and didn't respond, just picked up his radio and told his dispatch he was on his way back, in some kind of cop-speak that also didn't sound like cop speak, you know? "Dispatch, 78 is 10-15 with 415 and 148."

The radio crackled back a second later with, "78, check," and those were the last words spoken in the car until we pulled up in front of the station.

Having your paws cuffed behind your back for a twenty-minute car ride is no joke, even in seats designed for it, and for the last fifteen I was trying to find a way to get more comfortable. I ended up leaning against the door so my weight wasn't against the back seat, head pressed to the window watching the shadows flit across the brickwork, the stark and lonely billboards, the streetlights zipping by in a pulsing parade. Peco's not a bad city, I thought, except that it was on the wrong coast. It exuded a salty humidity that even our coastal cities out west don't have, a kind of mix of sweat and age and salt water, like someone had left the city out for the winter and was just opening it up again for the spring.

Only it was actually late summer now and even the evening air was humid enough to make me pant. So I looked pretty undignified when the tiger yanked the door open and I was half-lying on the seat with my tongue hanging out. "Evening, officer," I said. "Great driving. Very safe."

He reached down and grabbed my shoulder to pull me out. I stumbled a little, which helped with my intoxicant story, but managed to stay on my feet (with the cop's help). He steered me into the station, where I blinked against the white lights and Neutra-Scent smell.

The booking took a while and then another cop, a female rat, took down my statement. "Do I have the right to remain silent?" I asked.

"You're not under arrest yet," the rat reassured me. "None of this is official. We're just going to hold you because you were acting erratically."

"Erratically?" I put on a wounded air, which was tough with my paws still cuffed. "I don't know what you mean."

"You flipped off my car," the tiger growled. "With both paws. And then ran away."

"Yes, er, speaking of…" I rattled the cuffs. "Could I get these off? I promise not to cause trouble."

The rat nodded up at the tiger, and he walked around behind to release me. I brought my poor abused wrists in front of me and stretched my shoulders. "Now, I admit that I was a slight bit not in my right mind. My wife just left me, you see, for Gerald. He's a cop. So I wasn't very well disposed toward you. I'm sorry, officer." I tried to look contrite.

"What about earlier, when you were blowing a guy in the park?"

I blinked. "I have no idea what you mean. I was drinking with my friends and then they went to bed and I took a walk. I was upset at my wife and I saw your car and I…I lost my head."

"You seem very sober now," the rat said.

"A good run and the excitement of being chased will do that," I informed her. I was feeling pretty chipper knowing that Zeb had gotten away. Even if they charged me, I thought they had pretty flimsy evidence and I could likely talk my way out of it.

She exchanged glances with the tiger. "We can see if you're feeling more chatty in the morning."

"Am I being charged with anything?"

"You resisted arrest." The tiger glared down at me.

"I did not." I remained cool. "You said 'stop,' and I stopped. Then you knocked me down. With a little more force than was absolutely necessary, to be honest, and I'm not sure I'm not upset about my bleeding lip." I reached up and touched it. "But given my earlier behavior, I suppose I can make allowances—"

"Shut up." Tiger Cop leaned in menacingly.

"You're not being charged," the rat said, "but—"

"Then I will stay," I said.

That took them by surprise. "You will?"

"If it's my decision to accept your hospitality, then yes." I gave her a winning smile, the kind that said that if she was impressed by my forthrightness and my suave well-spoken manner, that maybe I could find time for her after I got done spending the night in jail.

"It isn't your decision, asshole," Tiger Cop growled.

She got up and pointed to the back room. "Officer Nagy will process you. Kendrick, take him back there."

"Yes, sir." The tiger gripped my shoulder and marched me to the back room.

"Do I get a phone call?" I asked.

"Call anyone you like," he said. "You're not under arrest."

We got to the door leading to the back room, and I wasn't sure what to do, so I reached out to open it. Before I quite knew what was happening, there was pressure at the back of my head and the door was coming up to meet it fast, and then stars exploded around me and pain throbbed through one temple.

"Fuck!" I said, probably too loudly, and stumbled back. The door opened, and Tiger Cop pushed me through.

Officer Nagy was a scruffy arctic wolf whose fur was coming out in clumps. He gave me a weary once-over as Tiger Cop said, "Drunk tank," and nodded.

"Though I'm not drunk," I pointed out, pressing a paw to my head where it still hurt.

"He fell into the door on his way in," Tiger Cop said to Nagy. "Busted up his lip too. Sometimes these drunk coyotes just don't look where the fuck they're going."

He turned to go, and I said, "Thanks for a fun night. Hope your gun doesn't accidentally discharge and shoot your balls off." The only answer I got was the smug smile of someone who knows he won, and the click of the door he'd smashed my head into.

"Jackson, what the hell," Matt said when I called his cell phone, as Officer Nagy typed in info off my ID.

"I guess Zeb got back okay." There was an old-fashioned wall clock over the desk. It read ten-thirty. Could it really be that early?

"He said he was being chased by police. What the hell were you guys doing? Where are you?"

I coughed. "Well, funny story. Along those lines…I'm in jail." There was a dead silence. "Matt? Hello?"

Officer Nagy looked up from the paperwork. "He's still there," he said. "They always do that."

"What are you doing in jail?" Matt sounded like he thought he was on a prank radio show.

I focused on Matt. "Well, the cops thought I was acting strangely so they brought me in and recommended I spend the night in the drunk tank. But I am not drunk."

"Uh, right. You sound drunk."

"That is…" I enunciated as clearly as I could. "Because my lip is a bit swollen from where the lovely police officer introduced it to the pavement."

He paused. "Jackson, were you…"

"What?"

He lowered his voice. "Were you jacking off in public?"

"No!"

"Then…" He paused. "This is…even for you…I mean…you're sure you'll be out tomorrow?"

I covered the mic and asked Officer Nagy, "I'll be out in the morning?"

"You can be out now if you want," he said. "No fur off my tail."

I glanced back at his ragged tail. "Is Officer Asshole going to come back and smash my head into the bars?"

The wolf grimaced and shook his head. I uncovered the mouthpiece. "Mm-hmm. Matt? Yeah, you can come by and pick me up in the morning."

"All right. We'll talk about it then."

I ignored the parental tone and gave him the station address. "So," I said to the arctic wolf as he got up, "do I get to choose my room or— okay, I guess I'll be in this one, then."

All the cells were empty, but he guided me into the one right behind his desk. "You want to be in a different one, you can make a lot of noise, and I'll put you down there in the one on the end that has the leak in the floor and the broken bed."

"Oh, this one will be fine." I inspected the drab cement block walls and the flat bed and the metal toilet. "Private bathroom, huh?" He snorted. "So do you guys just not get many drunks here?"

"Not on a Tuesday night."

"Right. I guess not." I walked over and stretched out on the bunk. "Believe it or not, this is an improvement over most of the places I've been sleeping lately."

Officer Nagy didn't seem to care much about that, so I tucked my tail under my thighs and stared up at the concrete ceiling. I'd spent nights in jail before, but I don't think I'd ever been quite so pleased with myself and sober at the same time. Why didn't more people take advantage of spending the night in jail? My throbbing head might have been the answer. I sighed and rubbed it, hoping the ache would go away by morning.

Day 19: Departure

It was weird waking up in jail without a hangover, though Tiger Cop's considerate gesture almost sufficed. But the sensation of having to go to the bathroom badly enough that I didn't mind peeing in front of my cellmates, *that* I remembered. Of course, I didn't have any cellmates, and Officer Nagy wasn't at his desk.

The noise of me moving around must have alerted him, because I'd barely finished before he poked his head back in. "Oh, you up?"

His fur didn't look any better. Clearly he hadn't spent the night combing it out. "I am," I said. "But my friends won't be here until eight and now it's…" The clock over their desk still read the same ten-thirty it had read last night.

"Six-thirty," Nagy said.

"Well, then." I smiled. "It looks like we have an hour and a half of conversation time to fill. So what—yeah, okay, I guess later then." I got the last bit of the sentence out just as the door clicked shut behind him.

There's not much to do in jail when there's nobody there to talk to. Maybe that's why more people don't just opt to spend a night there. Also the smell. That was much worse in the morning, for some reason.

I lay back down on the bunk and laced paws behind my head. An hour and a half alone with my thoughts. Should go by like *that…*

🎸

"I always figured I'd have to pick you up at the police station sometime," Matt said as we drove away. "I just thought it would be for something else."

"Like what?" I touched my lip. It wasn't as swollen, but it was still tender.

I stared at him, waiting for the answer. "Oh, I don't know," he said after a while. "Petty larceny. Art fraud. Confidence games. Indecent exposure. Take your pick."

I leaned back in the seat. "I would never be arrested for *petty* larceny." Letting my head loll to the side, I tried to catch Zeb's eye, but he was staring down at his lap.

In front of me, Lars snorted, and his tail tip flicked. "At least you're feeling better," he said.

It wasn't until we'd gotten to the neighborhood of the club that Zeb and I got a little time to talk. Matt had dropped us off at the club with instructions to go inside, find the manager, and not do anything that might get us in trouble with the police. He appended my name to that last one, which I figured I would let slide for another day or two.

Anyway, we found the manager, and Lars checked the acoustics while Zeb and I unpacked our stuff in the cramped dressing room. Since he wouldn't talk, I said, "Are you okay?"

"Yeah," he said. "Sorry I've been quiet."

"I'm sorry we got chased by the police," I said.

"I'm sorry you got caught." He brushed his fingers across the strings of his bass and started tuning it. "And…a little surprised."

That was promising, anyway. "Why surprised?"

"Well…" Now he looked up. "You're always going on about how clever you are. I'd have thought you'd be able to avoid them."

My goodness, my heart skipped a beat. It was definitely time to modestly acknowledge my sacrifice. "I could have, I'm sure, but then Mister Tiger Cop would have chased you."

"Wait." His eyes gleamed, focused on me. "You…distracted him? To save me?"

I ducked my head and smiled. "I must admit I got a little pleasure out of this." I repeated the double middle finger I'd given the cop, making sure to aim it well away from Zeb.

"Oh, no, you're joking." He looked aghast as I shook my head. "Jackson, why?"

"Well, I figured I could talk my way out of it—and I did, as you note. All it took was a little intoxication and some sympathy for my divorce and they allowed me to stay the night." I didn't mention the headache, which was now almost gone anyway.

"Well, uh." He rubbed at his muzzle. "Thanks. I mean, if they'd caught me, I probably would have…I don't know what I'd have done." His ears lowered and his eyes dipped to his own groin. "Wait, they didn't charge you for, uh…the park…?"

"What park?" I said innocently.

He smiled. "I don't even know if I'd have been able to lie."

"Clearly you need more practice," I said.

"I don't know that I want to lie better." He finished tuning the bass and strummed a chord.

I did the same with my guitar, and then I heard Lars stop singing and claws tap-tapping along the hall, so I gauged Zeb's mood and took a chance. "I didn't necessarily mean lying."

He had time to look surprised before Lars came back in to tell us that the acoustics were terrible because the place was a hundred years old, but we'd muddle through somehow. "It's fine," I said. "We have some practicing to do anyway. At least they're used to bands sounding like they're in a hundred-year-old pit. It won't matter much if we're a little out of practice."

"We're not out of practice," Lars said, and then looked at me. "Unless you're rattled from your time in jail."

"No, I'm fine, thanks. Better than ever, in fact. I've hardly thought about Jazmyn all day."

"Really?" Zeb left off strumming his chords.

"Yeah. I mean, I'm still thinking about her enough to know I'm not thinking about her, but it's not as bad as it was yesterday."

"Think you can get through a show?" Lars asked.

Anyone else would have said that sarcastically, but Lars doesn't play that. So I bit back the snappy answer and just nodded. "All right," he said. "I know I have to work on keeping my composure."

"No, no," I said. "If you're going to be a lead singer, you have to be a diva. I'd be disappointed if you hadn't stormed offstage at least once on this tour."

He put paws on his hips and glared. "I have never done that before! I was just on edge, and we were messing up…"

"I was messing up. It's okay, you can say it."

"Well, you're going through a divorce." Even when I was ragging on him, he still had sympathy for me.

That was about as far as I could go in teasing him. "I'm better tonight," I said, and shot Zeb a glance in case he was watching, which he was. He caught my meaning and his ears flicked about.

"Good," Lars said. "Whatever's helping you get over it, just keep it up."

I did not look at Zeb as I nodded. "I'll do the best I can. Being with you guys is helping out a lot. I mean, the theory the other night was that I could lose myself in the music, and I think that's still the best idea."

That was the theory, anyway. When I came out onto the stage and started playing, though, I tried to get into the zone of the songs and I just couldn't. My head still hurt a little bit, and that got me into my head thinking about Zeb and then about Jaz, and then about Jaz and

Gerald again, and I fucked up a chord. Then I got paranoid about it, over-cautious, focused on the music, got through a second song, and completely futzed the opening of the third. Like, we had to start over.

Lars didn't fall apart this time, though. Maybe he was ready for it, or maybe it was just that he loved "Losing My Religion" and I could've punched him in the back and he'd still have sung it perfectly. Zeb noticed and glanced worriedly my way. I gave him a thumbs up to indicate I was getting it together, and I went on through the rest of the show without fucking anything up *too* badly.

We left the stage to scattered applause, but I had the feeling of being on the edge of a cliff the whole time, barely balancing well enough to stay on my feet. It was a relief to collapse into a chair in the dressing room.

"Well," I said as Matt came in after me, "that coulda gone worse, am I right?"

He closed the door, and then I registered his down-curled tail, his flat ears, and the fact that Lars and Zeb were staying outside. "Hey, Matt," I said in a jokey-dopey voice, "what's the rifle for?"

It didn't defuse things the way I'd hoped. He sighed and slumped against the door. "Look, Jackson, we all understand it's hard with the divorce, you know? But when we get up to Port City, there's a couple record labels who'll be at our shows, and we need to sound professional."

"It's not going to happen again. I got it under control."

"That's what you said last time." Matt brought both paws up and pressed them to the sides of his muzzle, closing his eyes.

"I mean it," I insisted. "You see how I finished out the set? I was fine."

"We can't risk it."

What he was saying started to sink in. I mean, I never thought he'd kick me out of the band, but it would've been impossible for even a sheep to miss what he was saying, let alone a coyote. "Whoa, Matt. I'm part of REMake."

"You are," he nodded, "and you will be again in a week or so when you've settled down."

I stood up. "I *am* settled down," I said. "You want to see me un-settled down, just keep up with this kicking me out of the band bullshit."

"Jackson." He put one paw out toward me. "We're not kicking you out."

"Damn right you're not. I founded this band with you."

Matt stayed in front of the door. "It's just a hiatus. Take some time off to get your head together."

"No!" I got right up in his face. "I'm not quitting."

"You don't have a choice." Matt's nose was an inch from mine, his eyes locked on me. "You're not going on stage in Port City."

"How are you gonna stop me?" I knew I was out of control, but I didn't care. First Jaz, then the band…soon I wasn't going to have anything left.

He sighed. "Don't make this harder. You know we can stop you."

"You know I can fuck up your entire gig. How are you going to play for a label guy without a guitar, anyway?"

"Zeb can handle the guitar. There's a guy I know in Port City who can play bass."

"You can't keep me away, Matt." He looked away, and I realized what he was intending. "Oh, no. No no no no no. You are not leaving me in fucking Peco."

"What the hell else are we going to do, then?" he yelled, driving me back a few steps. "You threaten to sabotage our gigs in Port City, I can't imagine what you'd be like riding in the van."

"So what? Where am I going to stay? Here?" I waved to the dressing room, which was full of cases of beer and boxes of liquor, napkins and broken glasses. "Out on the street?"

"We asked around. There's a hostel you can stay at for cheap, and then you can take the train up and meet us in Freestone…I guess…or we can swing by after Freestone and pick you up."

I could see the hostel room, barely different from this little barroom closet except that it would be stacked with bunks and cots and smelly people who couldn't afford hotels. Like me. I'd be there alone, with nothing to do but brood about Jaz, about my music, about my future.

All the energy left me. I slumped against the shelf next to Matt. "Don't leave me in a hostel," I said. "God. Please."

"You can't play with the band." He wouldn't look at me, and I knew he hated saying it as much, or almost as much, as I hated hearing it. The part of me that wanted to growl and snap still raged, *then why is he saying it?*, but I knew I would've said the same thing to him if our positions were reversed. And likely I would've been more of an asshole about it.

Fuck self-awareness. I hate it. "I won't play with the band," I agreed. "I'll just, I'll find somewhere to go and sit and I'll stay out of your way." My tail was curled between my legs tight enough that I could feel it on my sheath. I felt like a cub again begging Mom not to leave me at home when she went on her shopping trips.

Unlike Mom, Matt relented. "Okay. But the first sign of trouble…"

"No trouble," I said.

"That includes jerking off in front of Zeb."

"I—" Zeb was a whole other problem. "Yeah. Okay."

"Because none of us can babysit you. You're going to have to be a responsible adult."

"I'm divorced, not ten," I snapped.

"I can't tell the difference, the way you're acting." His voice got sharper too, and then he closed his eyes and took a deep breath. "Sorry. Look, I'm going to tell Zeb and Lars and let them in, and if you want to stay, stay. If you want to go to the van, then go."

I was going to stay, but Lars barely looked at me, just went to his dresser (a low cardboard box). Zeb did the same, then turned around with his ears down and said, "Uh, hey, Jackson, you, uh, you okay?"

"Fine," I said, but I couldn't get my ears up and I didn't want to stay around making small talk, so I just walked out of the little room, which was too crowded anyway, and strode through the club. The sounds and smells of alcohol and the people drinking it battered at me with no effect. I reached the front door and pushed myself through it, found the van in the parking lot, and realized I'd forgotten to get the keys from Matt.

So I just slumped against the van and tried not to think about anything that had just happened. Would I ever really be able to play shows again? I had to believe the divorce contract wouldn't always be sitting front and center in my head, but right at that moment I didn't believe it. And what if I got into the habit of messing up songs and then couldn't break it?

And what about Zeb? The guy was cute, sure, and I enjoyed playing around with him. Was I just doing that to make up for Jaz? Was the divorce permeating every aspect of my life without me realizing it? And what did Zeb want?

Well, that last one I could ask him. I had probably won some points with him for saving him from the police, even if I'd lost some by fucking up on stage. The kid lived and breathed music, so probably he thought less of me for not being able to get through a couple simple songs.

Fuck. I pressed two fingers to my eyes. I had to get out of my head somehow. When I was married, I could—well, I wasn't married anymore, was I? There was nothing around the parking lot but hazy streetlights, everything closed except for one lonely convenience store. I didn't know where to find hookers here, or even a might-not-be-innocent massage parlor. I could get drunk, but that would take longer and last longer. And I couldn't afford any of that anyway. My total cash in pocket amounted to twelve dollars.

And then I looked again at the club.

Night 19: Drive

Twenty minutes later, I walked out with a bobcat in a tight red dress. "You canids don't like smoke, right?" she said.

"If you want to smoke, go ahead."

She took out a cigarette, held it between her fingers, then put it away again. "I'll save it for after."

I grinned and gestured gallantly. "Your place or the alley behind the bar?"

"Don't you have a motel or something?" Her interest dimmed.

"We sleep in a van that is shared by the rest of my bandmates." I put a paw over my chest. "Would that I could offer you more palatial accommodations, but…"

"Ah, shut up." She looked me up and down. "All right, fuck it, it's been like a week. Let's go."

She took off without another word, and I followed her three blocks past alleys that doubled as toilets and sparkling fields of beer-bottle glass to a second-floor apartment, a tiny studio. "Claire works nights," she said, gesturing to the lower of two bunk beds, "so don't worry about her walking in."

"Does that mean we're doing it up top?" I eyed the rickety frame.

She made a face. "Either that or on the floor."

We picked the floor so that we wouldn't have to worry about falling off, which it turned out would have been a real possibility. Her name was Tasha and she liked to be pretty active. She pulled me to lick and nip at her breasts, then went down on my cock like it was a popsicle in July before digging into a big box of condoms and grabbing a ribbed one to put on it. I lay back while she rode me to the end and then fingered herself with me locked inside her so she could come another two times, which I enjoyed from an aesthetic more than physical perspective.

When she was done, she pulled herself free and stood up, panting. "That was pretty good, band dog. I'm gonna go shower. If you want to clean up, you can stick around, otherwise I'll see you next time you're in town maybe."

What I wanted was to lie back and close my eyes on the thinly carpeted floor. If I waited long enough, Matt and the guys would just take off without me, and then I wouldn't have to deal with those problems anymore.

But I couldn't stay here with Tasha, and I didn't have anywhere else to go. So I pushed myself to my feet, grabbed my clothes, and kissed her on the nose. "Thanks for a good time, cat," I said. "I'll look for you next time I come around." I got dressed while she showered, then let myself out.

Outside her apartment building, I breathed in the cool urban car-and-piss-scented air and got my bearings, then trotted back toward the club. The closer I got, the more I expected to see the van gone from the parking lot, but I rounded a corner and there it was, with a dark-furred shape leaning in front of it. His little ears perked up when he saw me and before I got halfway across the lot, he was striding in my direction.

"Goddammit, Jackson," Matt said. "Where the fuck have you been?"

"Taking care of my libido. What time is it?"

"An hour past when we were going to leave is what time it is. Get in the van."

"I'll drive," I offered as I climbed in, and punctuated the offer with a huge yawn.

Matt got in behind me and headed for the back. "Fuckin' right you will."

So I took possession of the driver's seat and started her up. Zeb leaned over between the front seats and touched my shoulder. "You okay to drive?" he asked. "I mean…you need company?"

I pulled the van out of the lot. "Wouldn't say no to it."

As I guided us down the streets toward the highway, Zeb worked his way through the seats and plopped into the passenger side. He pulled the seatbelt across his chest and clicked it into place.

I snuck a look at Zeb, at his slender, delicate muzzle, at his large ears currently splayed out, and at that moment the kit fox turned his dark eyes on me. He smiled, and his nose twitched. "What were you off…" In mid-question, he paused and leaned a little closer. "Oh."

"I met this girl in the bar." My ears caught the creak of him settling back in his seat, even over the engine noise. When I flicked my eyes his way, he was looking out his window, away from me. "Hey, what's up?"

He didn't answer. I reached over and tapped his knee. "Zeb?"

His muzzle turned, nostrils flared. "I can smell her, that's all."

"Oh yeah, I guess…" Now that he mentioned it, of course I could smell her too. "Sorry, I didn't shower because I was a little tired."

"Are you okay to drive?"

"Why didn't Matt want to sleep in that parking lot?" The highway was nearly deserted. I pulled us on and got slowly up to speed. "I wouldn't have gone back to her place if I knew he was going to leave tonight."

"He's nervous about this Port City gig. He wants us to have time to rehearse...uh..."

I finished the sentence in my head: *without you*. I tightened my lips and nodded. "It's only a two hour drive. We can stop for coffee halfway."

"Sure." Zeb still didn't smile, but he appeared to relax. His tail uncurled; I hadn't previously noticed its tension.

After a while, I flicked my ears back and caught rhythmic breathing from the back. So I lowered my voice, turned up the music on the rear speakers (Gin Blossoms), and said, "Zeb."

He turned. "You feeling sleepy?"

"No. Just...remember when we talked about the end game for this cover band?" He nodded. "What do you think Matt wants to do with this label guy in Port City? I mean, I can't imagine a label wants to do an album of R.E.M. covers."

"Way I understand it," he said, "labels like to have studio musicians and tour musicians who can play certain styles. So if like Quentin Darby needs a backup band, they might call us."

"Or just a guitarist or bassist. Not a drummer, though."

Zeb shrugged. "Matt's not that bad. He keeps a beat."

"He doesn't do anything with the beat."

"Sometimes that's what people want."

I was quiet, thinking about that. "Are you going to take off with 'WTF Kenneth'?"

He rubbed his paws along his legs and didn't look at me. "I won't do your solo bit, if that's what you're asking."

"You could."

"Sure. But I won't. It's yours. I'll come up with something."

I hated thinking of someone else playing guitar with the guys, but what could I do about it? As much as I pretended I wasn't thinking about Jaz, she was always there in my mind along with her seventeen-page divorce contract and her Gerald, and I might be fine for a show but I might also break down again. "Knock 'em dead."

"Thanks." He lowered his head and his ears came down. "I wish you were playing with us. It'll be weird playing guitar."

"You can do it."

"I know I can do it," he said. "I'm just saying, it'll be weird. I like playing bass to your guitar."

"We kicked ass, didn't we?" He nodded. I decided to take a bit of a leap. "So…shifting keys a bit here…do you know what you want yet?"

He smiled. "Oh, I just want to keep playing the music. Something'll come along."

I listened to the back of the van again. Still asleep back there. I half-whispered anyway. "I mean with me."

"Oh." He looked down at his paws in his lap. "I don't really know. I mean, what do you want?"

"Fair enough, I guess. But look, promise me to be honest about what you want. Don't just say you want the same thing I say. Okay?" He nodded. "All right. The truth is, I don't really know either. Whatever I want is all clouded up with the divorce and everything. So right now I kinda just want sex, and you're extremely hot, close, and available."

His ears flicked and he murmured, "I'm not that hot."

"Oh, please. Allow the old expert in the field to assure you, my dear boy, that if you went to a gay club even dressed as blandly as you like to do, you would have to beat off your suitors—with a stick, I mean, not the way you so kindly did me the other night."

He smiled a bit and didn't say anything else, so I went on. "But you're also a great guy. I love playing with you, too. I don't think there's any reason for us to be talking about anything longer term than 'let's hang out after this tour,' right?"

"Oh, yeah." He nodded. "That makes sense."

"So…friends with benefits? Musical and otherwise?"

He turned his smile on me. "I'm cool with that. This is kind of a crazy time, but…you know, believe it or not, you've been a real help."

"Funny," I said. "We get interrupted every time I try to help you."

He laughed. "I mean, you're just so casual about everything. And you're married—ah, sorry." I shook my head to let him know it was okay. "I mean, you just took everything in stride and it wasn't a big deal. I was so worried early on that you'd just call me a faggot and wouldn't want anything to do with me."

I wrinkled my muzzle at him and jerked my head toward the back. "Uh, have you seen what Lars and Matt do together?"

"No."

"I mean—figuratively. Matt's one of my best friends and he's gay. Why would you think I wasn't cool with that?"

"Force of habit," he said quietly. "I mean, literally almost everyone else in my life except my therapist wasn't."

I tried to imagine that. My life had been a series of everyone telling me to do what felt good, from parents to friends to Jaz (oh Jaz), even past the bounds of the law sometimes. Hedonism was my guiding principle, and I lived my life by the precept that your appetites will take you interesting places and your brains will get you out of them. So far that Coyote Creed, as my mom called it, hadn't failed me. Until now, I guess, when my brain was struggling with the Jaz problem.

But even that wasn't because she'd told me I was wrong; it was about losing a part of my life. Now I set my brain to imagining what kind of life I would've had if everyone in it had told me that all my urges were wrong. That I shouldn't pursue music or ladies or boys or the occasional drugs. I would have graduated from college, probably. Probably wouldn't have married Jaz—a stripper from Vegas? But she made me feel good, and I'd thought there was the potential for more there. No; there *was* the potential. It just hadn't ever come to life.

Hey! I told my brain. We're thinking about Zeb here. Poor guy, living his whole life with people telling him that whatever made him feel good was sinful. "How did you get into music?" I asked.

"Oh." He frowned slightly. "Singing was encouraged, and I wasn't bad at that, but I liked playing guitar. So I was allowed to do that, and then a few of us in college formed a band. I liked bass because it was in the background but it was still important and challenging. You could do things with it that people would hear and appreciate without necessarily noticing."

"Uh-huh." My mind skipped around again. "But none of them was gay."

"No." He scratched his cheek ruff. "Actually, uh, the reason I auditioned for you guys was because one of them saw the board you listed on. We don't play anymore but we keep in touch. He sent an e-mail saying that there was a board for, uh…" He made air quotes. "'Faggot bands.' It, uh. It took me a week to get up the nerve to go and look. And I saw your listing there."

"Matt advertised on a gay band site?"

"You didn't know?"

"Nah, he just told us when we had guys come in for auditions."

"Oh." Zeb smiled. "Well, the ad just said the bassist had to be okay with gay people. And I thought I was."

"And you still thought I might call you 'faggot'?"

He shifted uncomfortably. "It wasn't really a thought, more like…a learned worry."

"Sorry you had to learn it. So you signed up for the gay band. What did you think it would be like?"

He coughed. "I didn't think anyone was going to, like, do gay stuff in front of me. And my therapist thought it was a good idea because there would be music, and I could hide myself in the music if I wanted."

"What did he? She?"

"He."

"What did he think about spending a month in a van living with two gay people and a bi guy?"

"Heh. Well, I left out that part."

I came up on a semi and passed it. The roar of the engine filled our van for a moment and then died away. "Aren't you supposed to be completely honest with your therapist?"

"Yeah, but...you ever been really scared to do something but you still really wanted to, and you knew that if you had just any tiny excuse you might not do it?"

"I'm sure I have, but nothing's coming to mind." I gripped the wheel. "Sorry. That was kind of flip."

"Nah—well, yeah, but that's what I like about you. You see a thing, you want to do it, you just do it. I'm trying to learn how to do that."

"Doesn't seem that hard to me." I indicated a sign for a rest stop. "You need a break?"

"I'm okay."

"But yeah, I guess I never had people looking over my shoulder and judging me all the time. So I'm glad to help you out." I watched the road over my paws. "And trust me, speaking as someone who's lived his whole life this way, it doesn't always work out. So maybe don't learn every lesson from me."

"Yeah," he said. "I'm sorry."

"Not just the divorce. I mean things like..." I flicked an ear back. "The whole thing about me being inappropriate on this trip. I'm sure that factored into Matt's thinking about keeping me off stage at this upcoming show. He knows I'm unreliable that way so he's not inclined to give me the benefit of the doubt. If you screwed up two shows but told him you had it together, he'd believe you."

"Oh." His lips tightened and ears went back.

"Hey, don't worry about it. I mean, I probably am the least reliable member of the band."

"You never stormed offstage in the middle of a show."

I waved a paw. "If a lead singer doesn't do that at least once, nobody takes them seriously. No, Lars is great and Matt's great."

"You're great." Zeb leaned over to me, intent. "That whole 'unreliable' thing, that's my fault."

"How the hell is it your fault?"

"Because I let you take the blame!" he hissed. "All that stuff they think you did is because you were covering for me."

"Not me fuckin' up two shows." The industrial wasteland south of Port City rose around us. I squinted at a road sign: 52 miles to Port City.

He slumped back into the seat and rested his paws in his lap. "Maybe if they knew the truth about the other stuff, they'd cut you more slack for that."

"Hey," I said. "Don't feel obliged to tell all your secrets. I can handle Matt's disapproval, you know. Been dealing with it for years."

"I thought you guys were friends."

"Best friends. That doesn't mean we approve of everything the other one does. In fact," I took one paw from the wheel to place it over my chest, "I consider it my duty as a coyote to do things that Matt and the world in general disapprove of. Just to remind them that those things can be and sometimes should be done."

"Did he approve of your wife?" Zeb asked quietly.

My bravado took a serious hit. I replaced the paw on the wheel. "No. He came to the wedding, though. And to be honest, the reason he didn't approve of her had nothing to do with her being a stripper. Lots of very nice girls decide to take their clothes off in public. Some pretty nice guys, too."

"So...what didn't he approve of?"

"Her flirting with my best man."

Zeb digested that. "He saw it?"

"He lived it."

"Oh." He chuckled. "I guess she didn't get anywhere."

"Oh, she knew he was gay. I believe he told me she said, 'if you ever want to take a detour, you know where to find me.'"

"But you guys were open."

"Weren't always." A large factory came up on our right. "We tried the monogamy thing for a bit. But she was always looking around and eventually it was easier, y'know, just to let her have a fling once in a while." I steered around another truck. "Also, I mean, come on. Flirting with the best man at the wedding? It's hard to be crass and cliché at the same time. But that's my Jaz. Was my Jaz. Now she's Gerald's Jaz." A pang, a tightening of my heart, but already a little less. She was a whole country away.

Zeb shook his head. "I never know when you're being serious."

"I could just tell you, but that'd take all the mystery out of it."

"Are all coyotes like you?"

"Goodness, no. I am an exemplar of my species." I put the paw on my chest again. "Wait, am I to understand that you've never known a coyote before?" His ears went back. "No, not like that, I mean, I know you've never *known* a coyote before, but talked to?"

He shook his head. "I don't think I've ever met a Mormon coyote."

"We're not great joiners, it's true."

"And after college, well, I haven't made a whole lot of friends. Losing the Church, you lose a lot of your support group." He tapped his claws together, and his tail twitched behind him. "All of it, actually."

"So you were just…alone?"

"Well, no." He exhaled. "I mean, I had the band and all, but they were all still Mormon, just not, like, fanatical. But when I started talking to them about having doubts, they just told me to go back to the Church. And then my therapist hooked me up with an ex-Mormon group, but I can't talk to the band about them and I only see them a couple times a week. I'm afraid to go out with them in case I run into people I know."

"You're talking in the present tense."

He flicked an ear. "Hm?"

"You said, 'I'm afraid.' You're still afraid to go out with them? I mean, you're part of this band now, you know. None of us are Mormon."

His eyes lowered and he looked away, out the window. "I meant that I was afraid."

"Come on," I said. "I know what you said and what you meant. Have you not left the church yet?" Slowly, he shook his head. "But you called yourself an ex-Mormon."

"I am. I just…" He heaved a sigh. "Haven't quite told everyone yet."

The lights of the factory complex receded in my mirror. We sped on through a dark section of countryside, probably lovely in the daytime, now merely impenetrable blackness beyond the glow of our headlights. "You said this happened two years ago."

He nodded. "Well…that's when I started seeing the therapist. I was more and more sure I was gay and I had a whole mess of doubts. But I kinda made the decision when I agreed to come on this tour."

"Jesus Dog." I turned to him. "Why'd you lie about it?"

He squirmed. "I didn't know you that well. And I didn't want to make it a big deal, like 'oh, we have to be careful around the kid who's dealing with a loss of faith.'" He exhaled. "I guess it probably wouldn't have been a big deal."

I grumbled. "It would've been nice to know someone else was going through a big change in his life. Oh, put your ears up, I'm kidding. So you haven't told your old band?" He didn't respond. "Your parents?"

"I keep putting it off. I mean, can you imagine what they'll say?"

"Having never met your parents, I can only imagine in very broad terms." I waved a paw theatrically. "But surely it's something you'll have to do. Can you just keep going home for..." I paused. "Do Mormons have Christmas?"

"It's not just that. They're deep in the church," he said. "They might disown me. I'll get lectures about not ending up in Paradise with them." He took a breath. I started to say something, but he was clearly struggling to get it out, so I let him. "And...part of me still wants to."

"Isn't your therapist helping with that?"

"Yeah, some." He stared forward into the blackness. "I mean, watching you go through this divorce...imagine if you'd never known anything but being married, your whole life."

"Yep. I can see that." I sighed. "What do your parents think about this tour you're on?"

"Oh, they said it was good for me to get out in the world and have experiences." He grinned weakly at me. "Probably not the kind I've actually had."

"I disagree, with all due respect. I think the kind of experiences you've had have been extremely valuable. At the very least, your friendship has been. You've distracted me from Jaz, which has helped tremendously. And from a less selfish perspective, your experiences have helped you figure out what you want out of life."

"Maybe." I caught the swish of his tail behind the seat.

"Have you regretted anything? I know, I know." I held up a paw. "You're going to be polite and say 'of course not' to spare my feelings. But please be honest. I have all tomorrow evening to cry about it."

That at least brought a more sincere smile. "I haven't regretted anything," he said. "I, uh." He shifted in his seat. "Part of me kinda thought when I saw your ad that a band run by gay guys just, like...all had sex together all the time. And then I found out you were ma—uh, straight, and I just got frustrated. Especially when I heard the other guys. That's kinda why I was…doing stuff…that first night, you know?"

"I'm glad the experience lived up to your imagination. Sort of. Hey, you know, if you come out to Lars and Matt, maybe that orgy isn't off the table."

He glared at me, picking up at least then that I wasn't being serious, and shifted again. "I feel bad about keeping it secret."

"Oh, let's keep doing that a little longer." I glanced in the rear view mirror. "Matt has enough on his mind."

"If you say so. You know him best." Zeb followed my glance. "He might not worry so much about you if he knew, though."

And he'd be upset at me for letting him worry. "A few more days won't hurt. Let him get through these Port City shows."

"All right."

I turned on some music for the last fifteen minutes, which brought us through lights, more factories, train stations, and finally suburbs to a rest stop about ten miles outside the city. Zeb roused himself from his thoughts as I pulled off. "Need a break?"

"Well, yes, but also, we can't park in Port City itself. This is nice and close and probably nobody will bother us here." I shut the engine down and leaned back in the seat, folding my paws over my stomach.

Zeb reclined his seat and lay back as well. After a moment, impulsively, I stretched out one of my paws to rest beside his thigh on the seat. He dropped his paw into mine and held it gently, and that warmth accompanied me to sleep.

Day 20: First We Take Manhattan

Port City's not a bad place to spend a day or two in, if you can forget your divorced wife and the band you should be practicing with. The buildings soar above you, every one a living monument, glass and steel and stone in a harmonic hodge-podge. On this old building there might be a huge sign proclaiming the Masonic Hall; across the square, a state of the art video screen showing ads 24/7. Everyone walks with purpose, playing a game of chicken with the cars on the streets that surprisingly few people ever lose.

If you're a musician, you'll see street performers and bootleg album sellers, small smoky clubs and big music publisher offices, and you'll feel adrift in a tide of people with direction and purpose and a goal. But if you're newly divorced, you'll swim through the mass of people and remind yourself that your ex-wife isn't the only one out there. It's a city of possibilities, and it's easy to see why the people who live there think the world revolves around them. Here, it does.

And when you get hungry, no matter where you are on the island, there are little restaurants and shops on every block from all over the world, and you can find an organic, locally sourced sandwich place where a ham on gluten-free rye will cost you $18, then cross the street to a deli and get twice the meat and all the gluten for a third of the price. I found a little ethnic place run by red pandas whose kung pao chicken seared the taste buds off my tongue, and an old record store that I had to leave after twenty minutes because I couldn't afford to buy anything and there was a find in every bin.

Fall hadn't quite taken hold yet; the day was warm and breezy, the girls were out in tight halter tops and short shorts, so just walking around the park kept me happy for a couple hours. I dozed off on a park bench until a cop prodded me awake; I managed to remain self-possessed enough to walk away with dignity.

The band had two shows scheduled on consecutive nights. The first night I managed to stay away from the club, but on the second night I decided that maybe downing the other half of the bottle of cheap scotch on the roof of the parking garage where we'd parked the van probably wasn't the best way to spend my second evening. So I stayed in the city proper and went to the club for the show. I could mingle in the crowd and the guys would never even see me.

Cellar Zero looked like a bar that had been hip back in the nineties, and the same could be said of its clientele. I was one of the five youngest people there, not counting the rest of the band and the bartender, and one of the other youngest people was clearly there with his parents. So it was a more sedate crowd and it wasn't hard to pick out the industry suit. For one thing, he was dressed business casual in a button down shirt and khakis, where most everyone else in the place was sporting colorful blazers over t-shirts that were either tour shirts for R.E.M. and other 90s bands or clothing brand shirts like Tommy Bahama. For another thing, he kept consulting his phone. Even the guys who were here alone didn't check their phone that often. And for a last thing, he was another of the five youngest people there, a cotton-tail rabbit with twitchy paws and whiskers he kept grooming.

So I went and sat near him, kinda back in the shadows in case Matt looked in his direction. It'd give me something else to think about when the band came out.

The pang I got when they did almost pushed me out of my seat and back out the exit. But I hadn't settled my tab yet, and besides, I was a coyote. I could take a lot more punishment than simply watching the guys play without me.

Matt made a brief announcement at the beginning about how the guitarist had been taken ill and the bassist was filling in, promising to deliver the same great R.E.M. sound. It occurred to me then to wonder why he hadn't gotten that guy he "knew" who played bass up here, if it was so important that we impress Mr. Bizness Cazh with the long ears. Maybe he didn't want to open the possibility that with an adequate bassist and Zeb on guitar, REMake would be offered a contract that would squeeze me out of the band. It was nice to think that Matt had altruistic motives like that, but the truth was that if a label guy told him he wanted Lars and Zeb but not Matt or me, then Matt the manager wolf wouldn't hesitate before signing.

So after the third song, my coyote nature got the better of me. "You ever see these guys before?" I asked the rabbit.

He grunted and didn't look around. "I know the guy on drums and the singer," I said. "Friends of mine."

His ears flicked around, though he didn't turn. "You the guitarist?" he asked. "Matt said he was a coyote."

"Sometimes," I allowed.

"Hope you get well soon." .

"Well, thank you kindly for those well-wishes. Can I buy you a drink?" I asked.

He hesitated, then finally turned. His brown eyes met mine. "It's not gonna affect my decision."

"Wouldn't dream of it," I said. "Just being companionable. We're both here alone, and I know you're working, but that doesn't mean you have to be bored."

"It's not boring." He tapped his phone, swiveling his ears back to the stage as Lars started in on "Drive." "Love this stuff."

"Glad to hear it. Then a drink from one music lover to another?"

He hesitated, then gave a curt nod and returned his attention to the stage. So I signaled the waitress for a refill of mine and his too, figuring I could put it on the band's tab. Then I thought that might not be kosher for him, work-wise, so I pulled out my wallet, but the five dollars left after buying the scotch weren't going to cut it, and this wasn't quite a big enough emergency to use the credit card, not if could come up with cash some other way.

In a moment, I had it: I'd just slip backstage and grab some from Matt when the show was over. There were two or three scams I could pull in a bar, but they all came with the risk that I'd get thrown out, and if I ruined Matt's show in front of Mr. Biz Cazh, well, that wasn't a trick a coyote pulled on a friend. Getting that friend to pay for drinks for shmoozing his record label guy wasn't even underhanded enough to count as a trick. Matt couldn't be upset with me.

In fact...what was stopping me from going backstage now and grabbing some money from Matt's wallet? I had the band photo that had the four of us in it in case someone stopped me.

Nobody did. I snagged two twenties from the wallet and then spotted a FedEx Express package on the table with my name on it. Curious, I grabbed it and hurried back to the bar. I couldn't tell from the return address who'd sent it, but it was from something called "Copper Realty" and they were located near where me and Jaz—or just Jaz, now—lived.

Ten minutes later I was back in my seat with a full G & T and a bit more swagger. During another break, I leaned forward to the rabbit, made bold because Matt seemed to be deliberately not looking in this direction at all. "So this is your second night watching them?"

"Yeah." He picked up his Tequila Sunrise, then looked back at me before touching it to his lips. "I'm not going to say anything to you, you know. If he sent you here to get info from me..."

I laughed and waved. "Perish the thought. Matt doesn't even know I'm here."

He considered that and then drank. "But you're sick?"

"Heartsick." I placed a paw on my chest. "Wife dumped me a couple days ago. I haven't been able to focus on music."

"Ah, shit." He rested an elbow on the back of his chair, turning toward me. "I should be buying you a drink."

"Wouldn't say no after this one." I toasted him and sipped the dry alcohol. "So look, you don't have to tell me what your verdict is, but I'm just curious…if you're impressed, what happens next?"

"Well…" he paused, swirled his drink, and took another sip. "Look, honestly, even if I recommend we sign him, Bob—my boss—has to figure out where he'd fit and what projects we have for him."

Him? I nodded, trying to parse that. So he was only interested in one of the band? That meant Zeb or Lars—and Zeb wasn't playing his usual instrument. Besides, if a record label signed Lars, Matt would go along as his manager for sure. I took a shot. "He's got a great voice and command of the stage."

The rabbit hesitated, then nodded. "It's not that he's not good. It's— is he better than the other guys we have, do we have a fit for him, so on, so forth."

"Totally understand." I let the G & T wash over my lips, numbing my tongue with the aftertaste of quinine and juniper, and my eyes rested on Matt. So it wasn't about the band at all. It was about his husband, getting Lars to that next level of fame, and screw me and Zeb.

That wasn't completely fair. I mean, honestly, I couldn't fault him for anything he'd done except for not telling us. I'd been planning to move on or nudge him to do something different with the band anyway.

Biz Cazh bought the next round, which lasted us through the rest of the set. We chatted about music and about female fickleness (he was one of those guys who thinks the best way to deal with getting dumped is to talk about how shitty all girls are, which I didn't really want to do, but he was enjoying it so I just nodded and went along). And when I'd finished my third G & T, I dropped both twenties on the table, wished the rabbit a good evening, and walked out of the club to the train, the mysterious package under my arm, a nice buzz between my ears.

I was two blocks from the platform when the FedEx box started ringing. After dropping it on the sidewalk in surprise and wondering if I'd had one too many drinks, I tore it open and pulled out a brand-new iPhone, still ringing. I hit the green button and put it to my ear. "Hello?"

Jazmyn's voice said, "So you got the phone."

"Apparently. Did Matt know about this?"

"I called to ask where you'd be playing and he told me, but I didn't tell him what I'd be sending." She sounded smug.

"Well, I wasn't playing, but I got the package anyway. What can I do for you? How's Gerald?"

She exhaled sharply across the mouthpiece. "Where are you?"

"Port City."

"I know that. I sent the package to the club, remember? Where in Port City?"

I looked around. "110th and something. Market?"

"What hotel are you staying at?"

I laughed. "The luxurious Ford Suburban Towers."

There was a pause while she put her paw over the phone; I heard her voice muffled through the speaker, then the sound of typing. "There's a FedEx office at 107th and Garnet. Can you get there?"

"Probably. I'm a resourceful fellow. Why would I go out of my way to find a FedEx at this time of night?"

"So you can photocopy your ass. What do you think, idiot?"

"Jaz, I assure you that I can survive the rest of this trip without any more legal documents from good old Gerald—"

"Shut *up*!"

Her vehemence shocked my tongue into compliance. She went on, a little better controlled. "This isn't easy for me, Jackson. I want you to stay part of our life."

"Begging your pardon." I tried to keep ice out of my voice, with not very much success. "But it's almost certainly easier for you than for me. And I've no desire to meet the handsome, dashing Gerald who isn't as good in bed."

"You think you know so much. You think you're on top of every situation. Well, you—" She stopped to breathe. "Did you read those divorce papers? Or did you just sleep on them for a day?"

"I read them."

"So you saw the bit about the equity? About the prenup?"

"We don't have either of those. We don't have a cub, either, unless you count Chauncey, but I thought we hated people who call their pets 'feathercubs.'"

"We do have a prenup, now."

I leaned back against a brick wall probably four times as old as I was. "Jaz, the word 'prenup' comes from 'pre,' meaning before, and—

She didn't let me finish. "Gerald's giving me some land before the divorce is final, so that's equity we both own, and he's buying out your stake in it."

Even for a coyote, this seemed needlessly complicated. "Wait, so he's giving me money? That's—don't do that, Jaz. I told you, I don't need his charity. I don't *want* his charity."

"It's not a million-dollar lot. It's about fifty thousand. It's in some backwater part of Teton or something, I don't know. It's Gerald's way of dealing with feeling guilty about stealing away your beloved wife while you're on tour. He thought of it himself."

That last sentence was almost certainly not true. "Why on earth would he feel guilty?"

She exhaled across the phone, exasperated. "Because I made him. Listen, your twenty-five thousand is in an account at the First Union Bank, and we're sending a fax with the account information to you at this FedEx, only you'd better go pick it up soon before some unscrupulous clerk decides to claim it for himself."

"Wait what?" I spun around, trying to figure out what direction 107th would be.

"I'm joking, Jackson. I'm only faxing you the authorization letter. You also need the account number, and I'll read that off to you right now. You have something to write with?"

"No! Who carries around a pen?" I jogged down Market and found 109th. "I'll be at the FedEx in like five minutes. I bet they have one."

"All right. I'll call you back in five minutes."

"Wait!" Too late. She'd hung up.

What the hell was going on? Did Jaz think that twenty-five thousand would make up for the divorce? She didn't owe me anything. How had she bamboozled Gerald into thinking he did? Was this just another slap in my face, a big fat "don't worry about it" in case I'd forgotten that Gerald could just find twenty-five thousand dollars in the spare change in all of his tuxedo pants pockets?

I prepared a whole bunch of questions for her, but when she called me at the FedEx, all she did was read off the account number. I scribbled it onto a Post-It and shoved it in my pocket, and then she said, "Good night, Jackson," and hung up.

The fax was indeed a letter signed by Gerald that authorized me to take full possession of the account (number supplied separately, contingent on me showing id), but didn't say anything about how much money was in it. Jaz wouldn't lie to me about that, though, would she? It'd be an extraordinarily cruel joke if she did.

So I leaned across to the FedEx clerk and said, "Where is there a really nice hotel in this part of town?"

I sat back on the cushy bed with my back against the mound of pillows and put the phone to my ear. It rang, rang, and then Matt picked up. "Hello?"

"Hey, it's Jackson. I got a new phone."

"Oh. We just got back to the van. Where are you?"

"Little place called the Conrad. I decided to sleep in a really nice bed tonight."

Silence. "Oh—okay. New scam?"

"Sort of. I'll catch up with you guys tomorrow. Unless the record label wants to fly you and Lars out to Crystal City right away."

Longer silence. Matt cleared his throat. I waited. "How...?" he said faintly.

"I ran into this really nice rabbit fellow in the club tonight."

He sighed. "Listen. I was going to—I promise you, Jackson, I sent a demo of the whole band. I did. They only wanted to look at Lars. I thought I could just talk to him once he'd seen the whole band, but then you went and fucked it up."

"Oh, no. You do not put this back on me. You lied to me, Matt. You made me feel like shit, and all the while you were planning to run off and take Lars and go make music without me."

"I wasn't *planning* on it." His voice faltered.

"You were hoping for it, then."

"I was going to tell you. After Port City. And maybe it'd be nothing, you know. Maybe they wouldn't even want him."

I parsed that sentence. "They already told you they like him, didn't they?"

He exhaled over the mouthpiece. "You can still stay at our place. You can sleep in our bed if you want."

"Fuck you, Matt."

"Well, that's not off the table either, I mean, if it'd make you feel better."

"Is Zeb there?"

"Of course he's here." Matt sounded relieved at the change of subject. "I already told him. He's fine with it."

"Sure. What'd you tell him, that the guy came to listen to all of us but only liked Lars?"

"I told him the truth!" Matt's voice sharpened.

"Just put him on the phone, will you?"

"Why?"

I growled. "You broke up the band, Matt. It's none of your fucking business anymore. If you don't put him on the phone I'll just call him on his, no big deal."

"I didn't—I didn't mean to."

"It's fine. I've got no family and no band now, so maybe I'll finally have time to go make music like you told me. Now put Zeb on the goddamn phone already."

His tone got quiet. "Here he is. It's Jackson," he said more faintly.

Zeb came on the phone. "Hi. Where are you?"

"I'm in a swanky hotel room. I'd really like you to come share it with me."

Night 20: I Believe

I was in the bar when he arrived, but I hadn't ordered anything yet because I didn't know if he'd want to wait and have a drink or just head right upstairs. He looked around and found me before I even waved my paw, and came over to sit down next to me.

"This is a really nice place," he said, eyes wide. "How can you afford this?"

"I've come into some money." I fitted an imaginary monocle to my eye. "At least, I'm told I did. If I didn't, then my credit card company will be having some words with me. I might have to leave the country. So it's probably best that you don't ask too much about it. I assure you that it's all very legal and I'm reasonably sure I won't get a police officer smashing my muzzle into concrete again."

He smiled. "Let's hope not. So, good news about Lars, huh?"

"Yeah." I tapped the table, good humor ebbing. "Good for him. Hope he hits it big."

Zeb's ears folded down. "Matt said you were upset with him. He tried to get all of us signed, he really did."

"I've known Matt a long time. He's a good guy, and we'll stay friends, I'm pretty sure. But right now, if he were here, I'd buy him a drink just to throw it in his face." Zeb looked to one side and nodded. I reached out and patted his arm. "I don't want to talk about him. You want a drink, or want to go upstairs?"

"I want a club soda." He looked around for the waitress. "You want a gin and tonic?"

We caught her eye, and when we'd ordered, Zeb gave her his credit card. I protested, but he waved me aside. "You're paying for the room."

So I let her take his card, and when she was gone, he looked a little discomfited. "I appreciate the drink," I said.

"There's another reason I wanted to buy you a drink."

I tilted my muzzle and perked my ears toward him. He didn't meet my eyes. "Well, you said…a couple weeks ago we were drinking, and you said…well, you said if I bought you one more drink…"

I didn't remember what I'd said. "What?"

"You said you'd…" He flattened his ears.

"I'd?"

"Uh. Blow me," he whispered.

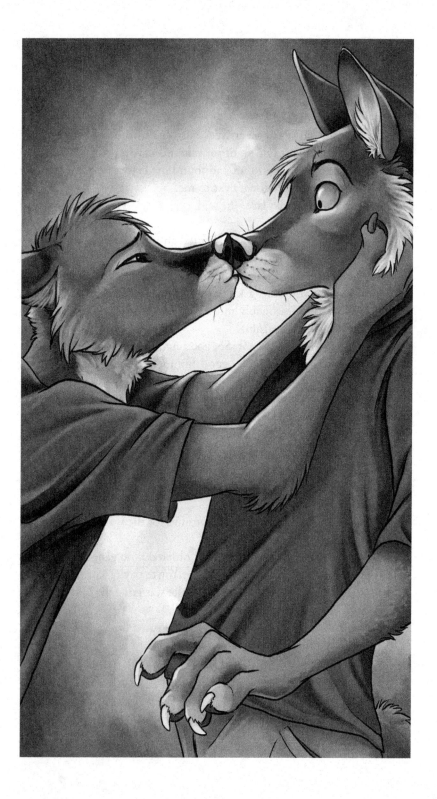

I stared at him and then laughed. "Aw, Zeb, you didn't have to buy me another drink for that. I was kinda figuring on doing that tonight anyway."

"Yeah, but…" He looked up at the ceiling. "We always got interrupted. I figured maybe if I bought you the drink, then that'd break the curse."

I squeezed his wrist. "I'm certainly willing to try."

After that, we made some small conversation, sipping the drinks so we didn't seem too eager to get up to the sex. Then when I took a longer drink, he finished off his, and I laughed and finished mine too. "All right," I said, pushing my chair back to stand. "Let's go."

So he followed me up, tail swishing, and I locked the door behind us while he gaped at the room. "Is this just a normal hotel room?"

"As far as I know. Nice, huh?"

He walked to the desk and the painting on the wall over it, then hurried to look out the window, which had a nice view of some of Port City's more scenic skyscrapers glittering as if the stars had come down to fill this little island and shine into our window. Haze hung between them, the humidity of an early autumn night, and above us, clouds reflected the light back down.

But Zeb didn't linger long over the view. He pulled the curtains shut and then turned with his back to them, covered the carpet between us in two strides, and pulled my muzzle to his.

Our tongues tasted like alcohol and desire. He made a small noise in his throat as I pulled his warm body against mine, sliding paws down his sides to link above his tail. His arms circled me as well, and we held the kiss and the embrace as I felt his hardness push into my thigh.

My paws found their way down his rear, and his held the base of my tail, and then our fingers worked their way inside clothes in a very enjoyable way, and then the clothes became bothersome and we pulled them down. I was ready to just lean in and lick him with his pants around his knees, but Zeb wanted to be completely naked, so while he stripped his clothes off, I followed suit. He brushed a paw down my stomach and teased my own erect shaft. "I think this is the first time I've seen you in the light."

I pushed him onto his back on the bed. "Later," I said. "Your turn first."

But as I lowered my tongue to his shaft and licked along it, he said something in kind of a low mumble. "Would you mmm mmm?"

I lifted my head, looked along the length of his lovely white-furred stomach and chest up at his worried expression. "Would I what?"

"Uh." He leaned back and looked up at the ceiling. "Get inside me?"

"What, now?" I brushed his shaft again, making him tremble. "Instead of a blow job?"

He nodded, and I crawled up the bed to lie beside him, my fur against his, and I rubbed his ears. "Well, we don't have condoms or lubricant, but I guess I could run out and get some."

"Oh." He seemed disappointed. "Well, can you…" His paw felt the warmth of my shaft, and it was my turn to shiver. "Can you just put this in me for a bit?"

I started to say no, but then I thought about it. My cock seemed to like the idea; I was not getting any softer thinking about it. I hadn't wanted to fuck him in that dressing room, but here in a nice hotel room, both of us naked instead of just pants down, it seemed much more appropriate. Matt had told me that spit worked for him and Lars when they were out of lube. And I could slide in and back out before I came, no harm, no foul, finish in my own paw or his. Worst case I'd yank myself out and come on his fur and spend a while apologizing.

I wanted to blow him, but if he wanted this more, then Jackson Alley would be there for him. Probably wanted to pop his last cherry tonight, and if it wasn't ideal, that was fine. We could do it properly later—maybe, if he still wanted to pal around with me after Lars and Matt took off. "You sure?"

He licked his lips again and nodded. "Yeah. I know it'll probably hurt. But…"

"I'll be gentle," I promised.

His slender muzzle nodded. "I know. And I—I trust you."

Ah, jeez, he was heading toward the "I want my first time to be with you." I touched my cock, expecting it to soften, but it surprised me by staying hard and excited. Did I want to be his first as much as he wanted me to be? What did that mean, if so?

I shook the thoughts away. "All right, foxy. Roll over on your stomach and hang on a bit."

He obeyed while I grabbed a couple washcloths, soaked them, and added soap to one. Back on the bed, I shoved a dry hand towel under Zeb's sheath and pushed his hips down. "Just relax."

"Mmkay." He was still trembling a little.

"I'm just going to clean you up first." I applied the soapy washcloth to his rear enough to make him squirm, then washed the soap out of his fur, and then dried it as best I could. He panted a bit but kept still.

I licked my paw and started to slicken him up, which made him gasp and moan, and at the same time ran my paw over his rear and tail, trying to get myself excited. Then it occurred to me that my cock would probably have to be slickened up again, and that process could serve two purposes.

So I moved around in front of Zeb and told him to suck until I was nice and slippery, and he obliged. Actually I let him go a little longer than necessary and then stopped when I felt like I was getting too close to finishing. One last slick pass with my fingers under his tail, and then I rested my cock there.

He tensed all up. I put my (non-licked) paw on his rear. "Calm down," I said. "I'm not gonna finish in you, I promise."

"No, it's okay," he breathed. His paws were fists holding on to the sheets, his muzzle buried in the pillow.

"I mean, seriously, relax. As best you can."

He tried, but still felt pretty tight. Things weren't getting any slicker, though, so I pushed gently into him.

I'd never done this before either, strange as it might sound, so I wasn't sure if it was normal for him to be so tight. But the saliva did its job and soon enough I was in all the way up to my knot.

I don't know what I'd expected it to feel like—like being inside that bobcat the other night, maybe. But it was different, and not just the physical sensations, which were tighter in some places and looser in others. It was the tension in his skinny body below me, the scent of him reminding me of jamming with him in the park, talking with him about our music and his religion, running away from the cops. Here we were safe, both of us, and we were as close physically as two people could be.

Without really knowing why, I lowered my body atop his, resting some of my weight on his back and circling his chest with one arm, then another. His tension and trembling slowly eased. I brought my muzzle to his ear and nuzzled it gently. I wanted to protect him—well, no, maybe that, but no more than a friend protects another friend. We were sharing this experience, guiding each other.

"How's that feeling?" I asked.

He grunted softly, so I kept talking. "I can't go any farther in. Is this enough?" His ears bobbed up and down. I slid my hips out an inch and then back in, but already our makeshift lube was drying. "How long do you want me to stay in?"

"Uh," he said. "I guess…as long as you want…?"

"I'm doing this for you." I wiggled around a bit. "Is it uncomfortable?"

"No." He exhaled. "I mean, a little."

"Well." I pushed my nose against the back of his neck. "If you wanted to have a guy's cock inside you…you've done that. If you want a guy to come in you, that'll have to wait 'til tomorrow night."

"No, it's okay."

So I slid out and used one of the cloths to wipe off my shaft. Wasn't even close to finishing, it turned out. Even when I lay next to him and pressed my cock into his hip, I felt good, but not, y'know, urgent. "Big night for you, huh?"

He didn't answer, just kept his muzzle buried in the pillow. I put a paw between his shoulders. "You okay?"

"Mmmf."

His body language was tense again, his tail curled and his fists twined in the sheets. My fingers rubbed at his shoulders. "Hey, so…I mean, I know first times are kinda weird, but…you can talk about it with me, right? You know, it was my first time doing that, too."

His back rose with a deep breath and then he exhaled into the pillow. "Dunno," he murmured.

"Come on. I told you about my divorce, you told me about your religion. There's not a lot you could say that would shock me, and I promise to be a good listener." I riffled claws through his fur. Part of me'd hoped that he would've felt the same thing I did from me being inside him, but there was obviously other shit going on. After all, he'd asked me to be his first, and we hadn't really done anything, so I couldn't have been unsatisfactory.

He sighed and turned his head, though he didn't get up. His eyes looked right at my chest. "It's…I know I left the church behind and all, but…now it's like, I've crossed a threshold. I've done stuff. I've done all the stuff. I—if I wanted to go back now I'd have to—there'd be a disciplinary council—I mean, it was all theoretical before."

"I thought you were done with the church." I reached around to rub between his ears.

"Not officially. Now I'll probably be excommunicated. Or something."

"If they find out."

He squirmed around to snuggle up against me, resting his head against my side and draping an arm over my stomach. My tail wagged, but his stayed lifeless. "That's the thing, though. I can't lie. If I try to go back to the church…"

"But you didn't want to." I was having a little trouble with this.

"No. I still don't. But you know, my family's part of it and I always sort of thought I could. If things got really bad, you know, or if it turned out…"

I slid my arm down to hold him closer and he made a soft contented noise. "If it turned out what?"

"That I was wrong."

I leaned over and nuzzled his ears. "Look, kid. I don't have all the answers by any means. I mean, my life isn't exactly a model of—anything really. But it is my life. Anyway, that's not the point, the point is that I think you have something great to believe in, and that's your music. You know, Hendrix said, 'Music is my religion.' Maybe he was onto something."

"It's easy when you're as good as he was." He sniffed into my fur.

"Yeah." I slid a paw down his ribs, ruffled through the fur, drew it up and smoothed it down. "I think you can be pretty damn good, though." When he didn't say anything, I said, "And look, if you want, you can come crash with me at Matt's place. I'd love to jam with you, work on our music together…I mean, I want to get way better at writing songs."

He looked up and rubbed his eyes. "And other stuff?"

"Well, yeah, and other stuff…you know I'm not looking to settle down with a guy, right? But sure, as long as neither of us is committed to someone else, I'm happy to continue adding to your experience."

"No, I know." His ears drooped a little, only a little.

"Hey. If I was looking for a guy, you'd be top of my list."

"Jackson," he said. "It's okay. I don't love you."

"I didn't think—"

"It's more that…you know, I'm gay." He stopped, listened to how that sounded. "I'm gay, and I liked being with you tonight, and I really appreciate you making me feel better about the church. Sorry for freaking out. But I want to get to know other gay guys. I still feel like you're only doing this for my benefit, not because you really want to put my, uh, dick in your mouth."

I pulled him closer. "First off, I like putting your cock in my mouth. I'm not just a straight tourist here. You've got a nice cock and I haven't sucked very many cocks, but I'll suck yours anytime, whether or not you buy me a drink. Maybe even tomorrow morning. Probably, come to think of it."

"Okay." Finally, finally, a little smile.

"Second, I want you to get to know other guys. Somewhere out there is a guy who's amazing and just right for you, who appreciates your music and is totally gay and wants a life with a cute kit fox. So if you're okay making music with me, and going to see bands in clubs and fucking at night when we don't have dates, I mean, that sounds like an okay life for a little while."

"You sure?" His paw rubbed up and down my stomach.

"I'm not sure about anything. But I'm a coyote. I follow my nose and just go."

"Okay." He exhaled across my fur, and then his paw trailed down to my sheath. "You want me to...uh?"

I nuzzled his ears again. "You know, you'd think I would. But I think I'm actually okay for right now. In the morning...." I let my tongue flick out along my lips.

"I'd like to do that again too." His fingers moved back up to my stomach. "I liked it when you were inside me."

"You said that."

"I know, but...I really liked it. I mean, that it was you, too. Because I trust you."

I smiled and licked his nose. "I liked it too. We'll get condoms and lube tomorrow, I promise. So you want to keep hanging out with me after tonight?"

He giggled and rested his head on my shoulder. "Well," he said, "I don't think I have anyone else to hang out with, so I guess so."

"Coyotes are fine, even proud to be someone's last resort."

He poked me. "You have money now, you said. So we don't have to stay at Matt's. Would you consider moving to Stilltown? The music scene there is great and I've always wanted to visit."

"I guess I do have money. But Stilltown...the music's awesome there for sure." He was closer now, and I could reach down to his butt, so I did. "The gay guy scene...not so much. What about Pelagia? Great music scene, great gay nightlife..."

"I could do Pelagia." He smiled again.

"Okay, well, first thing is getting back home. We could fly back with a stopover in Stilltown?"

His soft laugh bounced him against me. "How much money did you come into? And how, for that matter? Can I ask that now that we've... that you've..." I waited, but he was just getting sleepy, not nervous about saying it. "Been inside me."

"My wife." I stroked his ears. "Soon to be ex-wife. Her new husband is pretty wealthy, I guess, and she's sending me a pile of money. It's enough to take care of two..."

"That's nice," he murmured, and then we fell silent, him because, I dunno, he was imagining Stilltown, or shacking up in Pelagia with a handsome coyote. Me, I was thinking about something else, something that had just clicked in my mind that very moment.

The best way for a clever coyote to get someone to believe a lie is to lead them to it by telling them nothing but the truth. Jaz and I had known each other long enough to smell out lies, of course. And I was thinking, then, of all the things she'd said to me over the last few days, and the one thing she hadn't:

The cub isn't yours.

She'd said Gerald wasn't better than me. She'd said it was just timing, that he was there and I wasn't. And I thought about a stripper getting past her prime years, finding out she was pregnant while her dreamy musician husband was on the road. I thought about her getting the call that we were going to the East Coast for who knew how long, wondering what sort of father her cub would be growing up with, or not growing up with. And Gerald, probably one of those coyotes whose cleverest days are behind him, or else he's a genius with real estate and not so smart with girls; older, very well off, and probably ears over paws in love with my gorgeous wife. Jaz was clever enough to muddle the timelines, and coyotes all look pretty similar (unlike, say, foxes); Gerald would always think the cub was his. He'd give them a better home than I ever could.

Jaz had said she wanted me to stay involved in their life. Not hers and Gerald's. Hers and our cub's.

As I was thinking about this, Zeb slipped into that comfortable post-coital sleep that is so often mocked in guys because it happens so often. His breathing became even and his muzzle lay against me and he was still smiling. I felt good about that.

But I wasn't quite ready to sleep, not quite yet. So once he was relaxed, I eased him gently to the bed, turned out the room lights, and padded to the window. Between the curtains and the world outside, I stood and looked out again at the city below. I was naked, still partly erect, but the room was dark and I was pretty sure nobody could see me from the outside.

A cub; the thing I'd thought was missing from my life. My impulse was to run back to the West Coast and be with Jaz. But I'd already signed the documents—including, I remembered, a custody agreement I'd thought was just cruel taunting—and Jaz had maneuvered me perfectly into the right situation. I hated it, but I had to admit I probably wouldn't be the best dad right at the moment, especially when I looked at it from her perspective. That perspective made me want to prove her wrong, but at least I was mature enough to realize I needed to work on it, and that'd take time. Besides which, it's coyote nature to appreciate a good trick, even when you're the one being tricked.

I would become a good dad, though, I vowed. Even if the cub never knew I was his or her father, even if I was just weird Uncle Jackson, I would start to settle down. That didn't mean I'd stop chasing tails here and there. It meant I would get serious about my music.

That's what Jaz's money meant. It wasn't an apology for the divorce or a payoff for the cub—well, maybe a little of those, but they weren't the main reason for it. I knew it as clearly as if she'd told me: "Here. You've got enough to live on for a couple years. Figure your damn life out."

Zeb would help me with that. He couldn't help me pick up girls in a bar, but he could get me something much more valuable. In the reflection of the window through a crack in the curtains, I saw the kit fox's ears and the curve of his smile superimposed on a skyscraper topped with bright blue lights. It was a big world, full of places for a couple outcasts to roam. We'd both got families we could check in on from time to time, but we'd be building our own lives for a little while. Port City, Stilltown, Pelagia, wherever. We weren't beholden to anyone but ourselves right now. It was a scary feeling, but if I thought about the possibilities, the freedom, the excitement, well, maybe it wasn't so bad. I put a paw to the glass and just tried to clear my head and appreciate the view and Zeb's reflection.

I felt as though the night were singing to me, a sad tune but one that contained hope, too, and a promise that the future was as big as the world. I closed my eyes to listen, and strangely, magically, the first chords of a song blossomed in my head.

About the Author

Kyell Gold began writing furry fiction a long, long time ago. In the early days of the 21st century, he got up the courage to write some gay furry romance, first publishing his story "The Prisoner's Release" in Sofawolf Press's adult magazine **Heat**. He has since won twelve Ursa Major awards for his stories and novels, and his acclaimed novel *Out of Position* co-won the Rainbow Award for Best Gay Novel of 2009. His novel "Green Fairy" was nominated for inclusion in the ALA's "Over the Rainbow" list for 2012.

He was not born in California, but now considers it his home. He loves to travel and dine out with his partner of many years, Kit Silver, and can be seen at furry conventions in California, around the country, and abroad. More information about him and his books is available at *http://www.kyellgold.com*.

About the Artist

Teagan Gavet is a professional illustrator, graphic novelist, and freelance rambler. Find more at:

http://www.teagangavet.com
http://www.furaffinity.net/user/blackteagan

About Cupcakes

Cupcakes are novellas, with more substance than short stories, though not as long as novels. The Cupcakes line was developed for FurPlanet by foozzzball, Kyell Gold, and Rikoshi as a reaction to their desire to tell novella-length stories and the lack of publishing opportunities for novellas.

Previous Cupcakes have been nominated four times for Ursa Major awards, winning twice, and four times for Coyotl Awards, winning twice.

About the Publisher

FurPlanet publishes original works of furry fiction. You can explore their selection at *http://www.furplanet.com.*

About This Book

"Losing My Religion" is the story of Jackson Alley, a coyote in an all-male R.E.M. cover band trying his hardest not to grow up. Tours, he feels, are for playing music and taking full advantage of the openness of his marriage, and having a gay wingman usually helped the bisexual coyote get girls. But his wingman is dating their lead singer now, so Jackson's left with the new bassist, an ex-Mormon kit fox named Zeb who might be gay, but knows as little about sex as he does about drinking. So Jackson's going to have to show him the ropes, and hopefully he won't have to learn any pesky life lessons along the way.

CPSIA information can be obtained
at www.ICGtesting.com
Printed in the USA
FSOW04n0518080517
33871FS